THE HOUSE OF POISON:
SWORD AND CRYSTAL SPARROW

ISBN: 979-8-218-83569-9
Published by Wild 7 Studios

This is a work of fiction inspired by historical events and figures. While certain characters, settings, and events are based on real history, the story as presented here is a product of the author's imagination. Any deviations from historical fact are intentional and used for narrative purposes.

The House of Poison:
Sword and Crystal Sparrow

Naz Red

To my father and mother.

"Gheisar, where are you? They killed your brother."

\- From the film "Gheisar".

Chapter 1: Murder Mountain

The fisherman's assistant was throwing up over the side of the boat, into an ocean that looked purple in the morning sun.

"Is this kid new to this?" Pirouz asked.

"He's my nephew," The fisherman said. "His mother just died. His dad's been dead for a while too, so he's become an apprentice of sorts." He laughed and added, "A weak-stomached apprentice." Pirouz leaned back on the other end of the boat, which creaked and would've splintered the back of his head had it not been so damp. Pirouz was nervous but not showing it. Instead, he appeared to be comfortable with his feet stretched out, playing with the handle of his sword. "That is an interesting weapon, young man."

"Yeah. I found it," Pirouz said.

"You lie," The fisherman said. "You found that blade and *I* am the emperor," The fisherman added sarcastically. "That blade is from the House of Poison."

Pirouz did his best not to react to hearing those words. "I don't know what that is," He said. "Care to enlighten me?"

"Oh, you're good." The fisherman said, his one good eye squinting at Pirouz. "How do you think I lost this eye?" the fisherman said. "Before I settled on being a fisherman, I had many unsavory friends- and unsavory friends know about The House of Poison."

"Is that so?" Pirouz asked. "So, what is the House of Poison, old man?"

"You young people. Always thinking you can trick an old man like me," He pointed to his nephew. "*This* one is like that as well- I always tell him I am old, not stupid."

"I don't think you're stupid," Pirouz said with a shrug. "I just don't know what you're talking about. I apologize if it came off that way."

"Fair enough. Whatever your business is on Murder

Mountain, it's none of mine. Give me some of that jerky, and you could be royalty from another land for all I care."

Pirouz smirked and handed the fisherman some jerky, then leaned back on the boat's edge with his hands behind his head. "You're right, old man. I'm a spoiled prince, and I am going to Murder Mountain because nobody loves me." He kicked one foot over the other and tried to nap. Blood Orange Island was still several hours away, according to the fisherman. He drifted in and out of sleep for the rest of the trip, until the nephew shook him awake as the island came into view. Pirouz stood and stared. Even from a distance, the mountain was overwhelming—its temple perched at the very tip-top, as if defying gravity itself. The temple was green, glowing in the setting sun behind it.

"Many men have died on that island, you know."

"Yeah, I heard it's dangerous."

"*Dangerous?*" The fisherman roared with laughter. "That is putting it quite lightly, young lad."

"That's what I heard."

"'Dangerous' is what you call an animal or an act of nature. That mountain is beyond dangerous—it's a world of pure murder! I once knew a man who went and managed to survive to tell the tale."

"What tale did he tell? What did he go there for?"

"He went, like many, to steal the Savior Sword. Surely you have heard of it."

"The *Savior Sword*? No, I can't say that I've heard of such a thing."

"It's a sword made from the blood of 7,000 men!" the nephew shouted this excitedly.

"Care to explain how that works out?" Pirouz asked.

"An ancient warrior, who was also a swordsmith, made the sword from the metals in the blood of 7,000 men—he said the heavens commanded him to."

"How so? I don't get it."

"Blood has metal, boy. Iron to be specific."

"Oh, okay."

"If you kill enough men, you can extract enough iron to make a blade. According to legend, the ancient warrior did exactly that—he killed 7,000 evil men the heavens told him to, and forged a sword from their blood!"

"Hm. That's a very interesting story." Pirouz had heard variations of it back at the House of Poison from his shifus, but never told so simply. "I'm happy your friend got to live to tell the tale."

"Yes—minus an arm and a leg. He couldn't get past a woman near the waterfalls. She sliced off his arm and leg, said she only did that because she was in a good mood, and ordered him to go back. And she wasn't even anybody important there!"

"How did he go back without an arm or leg? Wouldn't he just bleed to death?" Pirouz asked.

"That's the funny thing—she cauterized the wounds herself and sent him back with a fisherman who makes rounds there to drop off food for some of the island dwellers. She even gave him wine!"

"Sounds like a nice lady," Pirouz said flippantly.

"I've seen women take more than an arm and a leg—so I suppose she was nice. The lady in the story? Dead. Everyone who goes to the mountain dies." He laughed at this. The rest of the boat trip passed in silence. Pirouz, the nephew, and the fisherman simply stared at the island and its mountain as they drew closer. Though his face remained calm, Pirouz was nervous. His stomach felt like a sack full of air. He kept his hand near his blade, gripping it tighter as the boat neared the island. "Blood Orange Island," the fisherman muttered under his breath. "So much death." The fisherman guided the boat toward a cluster of large rocks where Pirouz could disembark. "As much as I would like to stay and converse with you, we must be going. I don't want to die." A needle flashed past Pirouz's eyes, missing him and striking the fisherman square in the forehead—blood sprayed out the back of his skull. His plump body tumbled to the edge of the boat. His nephew jumped back.

Pirouz leapt onto the rocks, then looked back at the boy. "Go, now," he said. The boy scurried over, grabbed both oars, and began to paddle. He froze in terror at the sight of a man in tattered clothing standing atop the highest rock. Pirouz knew, from the glint of the passing needle, that he was already dealing with a dangerous member of the martial world.

"I am Jun Hei, master of the dragon, tiger, crane, and snake styles. State your name and business, boy."

"Jun Hei, did you have to kill that man? You could have asked him to leave first."

"Nonsense. All I see on this island are enemies." He used lightness kung fu to leap to the boulder nearest Pirouz. "I will destroy all who stand in my way, for I will be the true holder of the Savior Sword."

"Ah, so that's what this is about." Pirouz leapt to the next boulder. The two were now several feet apart on the same large rock. The waves crashed just to the side of both.

"Why else would one come to Murder Mountain?" Jun Hei asked.

"Personally, I have a few," Pirouz said, his eyes blank.

"Well, boy, I challenge you to a death match on these rocks—for I will not let you pass." "Okay, cool, but let me ask you something before we proceed."

"Certainly. I will entertain one question before I break you like a twig."

"You look like someone already roughed you up. Your clothes are tattered but made of fine fabric. Someone must've gotten to you first—and now you're stuck here. Am I wrong, old man?"

"Old man?" He laughed. "I'm but a few years older than you, little boy—and for your information, no warrior has bested me. Not yet."

"So you came here in tattered clothing?"

"The boat ride was quite treacherous."

"The waves were choppy, sure—but I wouldn't say they'd leave someone looking like a vagrant."

Jun Hei looked ready to explode. "A vagrant? Ha! You're

a mongrel boy, and you call *me* a vagrant? You should be ashamed of yourself! I am Jun Hei, holder of the Savior Sword!"

"You have the Savior Sword?" Pirouz asked.

"Of course I do not! The Savior Sword is at the top of the mountain—but it might as well be mine!"

"That's wonderful. I might as well own an elephant too."

"Your mocking tone will be the reason your death will be painful, boy."

"Whatever ripped you up left you with a bad attitude, old man. Please—tell me. I'm dying to know: who beat your ass?"

Jun Hei looked like he was fighting off embarrassment. "No one *beat my ass,* as you so crassly put it, mongrel."

Pirouz chuckled. "Mongrel," he said under his breath with a smile and a shake of the head. It was probably the millionth time he'd heard that word to describe him.

"I'll have you know why my clothes are in tatters—but know this: it's part of a larger plan, far beyond the grasp of a small mongrel mind like yours."

"Okay." Pirouz sat down cross-legged like a little boy waiting to hear a story. "I have time, tell me."

"There's an inn one must pass to gain access to the mountain. It is just several *li* away from here. "It's run by a rather awful woman who will only grant you patronage—and access to the mountain—if you can take the dumplings from her hands."

"So you tried and she whooped you like an animal and made you look like a bum?"

"You mongrel," he said, this time with a sizzle of hatred. "I allowed her to beat me—so I could study her tricks and ways."

"I see. But *why* did she beat you?"

"Because I let her."

"Oh come now. Be serious. You let a woman beat you up?"

"Yes, to understand her tricks and ways, like I said."

"Hmmm, that seems odd."

"Believe what you will. After I defeat you, I'll march back over there and show her a piece of my mind—in the form of my fist crushing her skull."

"Okay, old man—let's see if your dragon, crane, tiger, and snake style can beat my mongrel style," Pirouz said with a smirk. Jun Hei launched a flying kick, but Pirouz stepped aside and landed an uppercut to his foot, spinning Jun Hei midair before he landed standing up. Pirouz charged at Jun Hei with a lightning-fast flurry of Crane Break strikes. Jun Hei blocked each blow, then returned the favor, each one blocked by Pirouz in rapid succession. Sensing there would be no end to the exchange, Jun Hei unsheathed his saber. The sun shone against the curve of his blade as he held it up.

"No filthy mongrel is going to get in the way of me and the Savior Sword."

"That's where you're wrong." Pirouz drew his sword. "This mongrel is *absolutely* going to come between you and the Savior Sword." The two clashed swords so quickly that the blades sparked in a fire cloud with every clang. Pirouz found an opening and swung around, slicing his blade across Jun Hei's throat. The blood sounded like it was spraying from a leather sack full of liquid. Jun Hei dropped the saber; it cracked against the rocks and spun unevenly as it fell into the ocean. "It's nothing personal." Pirouz flicked the blood off his blade. "I just happen to have the same business here you do, apparently." He sheathed his sword. "So I'm afraid you're gonna have to die." Those were the last words Jun Hei heard before he fell to his knees, his skin now white. He slumped forward. Pirouz looked at the body. Every time he saw a throat slit, he couldn't help but think of his father—and how he'd seen him die that very same way, by the blade of a man.

Pirouz climbed the rocks, then turned to look at the ocean. The boy was now a few li away, struggling to paddle—his dead uncle slumped on the other side of the boat. He took in the sight, then walked toward a grassy stretch leading to a suspiciously plain-looking trail and an equally plain-looking inn Pirouz had heard about. He stopped midway across the grass, which stretched on briefly before giving way to the forest. Just ahead, he could see the inn. *Auntie's Inn,* the letters read.

Pirouz remembered:

Not more than three years ago, he was doing breathing exercises with one of his Shifus, Master Míngzé, in the courtyard of the House of Poison. When they were finished, Master Míngzé relayed the story of when he first went to the island, when he was just a few years older than Pirouz.

"There is a woman who lives on the island, she has lived there since she had a falling out with her Shifu many years ago. No one can go deep into the island without getting passed her. In order to go past the only bridge over the great water falls of the island, you have to cross her inn. I learned this all too well."

"What happened?"

"She beat me!" he laughed. "I was so young and foolish. I thought there was no way an older woman could beat me, but she *did* beat me, badly."

"How did you get passed her, then?"

"I kept going back, year after year, until one year I managed to land a single blow with the tip of my finger on her nose."

Pirouz had to ask, "Is the food good?"

"The dumplings are exquisite—probably the best I've ever tasted. Try them if you can!"

This memory flashed in Pirouz's mind as he took a good look at the inn. He thought to himself: *Should I call her out to a challenge? Or should I just go in and politely ask for dumplings? Perhaps I could charm her into just letting me pass.* He decided it best to just present himself by walking right up to the entrance which was covered with a pink cloth and stating his intentions.

"May I speak to the owner of this inn?" he shouted. A woman's head approached the pink cloth and pushed it aside, she gave Pirouz a scowling look. She was older then Pirouz's Shifus but seemed well preserved in her mature age.

"What do you want, boy?"

"I would like passage to the bridge across the waterfalls."

"Oh?"

"Yes."

"Do you know this is Murder Mountain, boy?"

"Yes, I am aware." Pirouz noticed a little girl preparing a bowl of stew that smelled heavenly deep into the kitchen of the inn, visible to Pirouz just over the innkeeper's shoulder. The little girl looked at Pirouz, then tried to ignore him as she stirred. "I am here on a special assignment from The House of Poison." The woman's face looked shocked when Pirouz said this. He continued: "Master Míngzé told me to send his regards."

"Where did the House of Poison find *you*?"

"Will you grant me passage?"

"Grant you passage? Ha! I first want to know how someone like you would even be accepted by those killers!"

"Madame, I am afraid it is very important you let me pass."

"I am sure that happy-go-lucky idiot Míngzé told you how to even gain a crumb of my respect..." The woman whistled to her young assistant, who looked up from the stew and picked up a neatly made plate of fresh dumplings and threw it at her so swiftly, it spun in the air and landed soundlessly on the innkeeper's hand. "If you can touch just one dumpling, not only will I grant you passage, but you can also have every dumpling you see. It will be useful for when you go up the mountain to be killed. You can bribe the killers with good food."

Pirouz looked at the dumplings, they made his mouth water with how perfect they looked, steam still wafting off of their glistening, creamy-white surface. They were probably the best tasting dumplings he would ever come across, an irony, being in a place as violent and ruthless as Murder Mountain. "What if I don't like them?" He said.

The woman's eyes grew. Her assistant looked shocked to hear that as well and looked scared of the aftermath of such careless words. "How dare you suggest anything I do is less than perfect! Who are *you* to question my skills in *anything*?"

"I'm not saying it would taste putrid, but it would be foolish of one to just assume you're the greatest dumpling maker in the world. I have had many dumplings madame. From the looks of it, these dumplings are, at best, the third best in the world. I think that is fair."

The woman scoffed at this. "There is nothing more pathetic than a stupid little boy trying to get a rise out of someone who has seen it all."

"I bet you have," Pirouz said with a grin.

The woman squinted, then spun the plate of dumplings on the tip of her finger. "If you can touch but one..." The dumpling platter twirled in the air to her other hand, spinning on her fingertip." Pirouz first tried to snatch a dumpling, using his snake style to fling his hand towards the tray, but missed when the woman flipped it behind her and caught it with the sole of her foot, kicking it back into the air, then bouncing it on her head, onto one of the tall trees hanging over the inn. Pirouz looked at the plate, then at the woman. "Forget the dumplings. If you can land just one blow, I will give you food for your fatal journey, so you can die with a full stomach!" She said. The two exchanged several swift blows, each one dodged by the other, before the woman leapt into the air, facing forward with a squint in her eyes. She could tell Pirouz was more skilled than she had assumed.

"Can we just keep it at touching a dumpling like you say then? I will be honest, they smell good."

"Fine, whatever. I just want to crush that smug aura of yours."

"Good luck with that!" Pirouz said. He raised his hand and pressed down on his wrist strap, releasing a needle from the tip of his knuckles, a needle that flew towards the young girl in the inn. The needle hit her in an instant, leaving behind a glint of light as it flashed towards her. The girl had a dumbfounded look on her face. She stepped away from the counter, then fell, knocking over one of the tables. The woman used her lightness kung-fu to swiftly drift back into the inn. Pirouz used this as an opportunity to calmly walk towards the tree where the dumplings were dangling. He punched it, causing the dumpling tray to fall. He caught each falling dumpling as they rained down, catching the last one with his mouth.

"YOU SWINE!" The woman cried out, tapping the young girl on the face. "WHAT WAS ON THE TIP OF THAT NEE-DLE?"

"Well..." Pirouz made himself a nice little spot to sit down under the tree, placing the dumplings back on the tray while he gobbled up the one in his mouth. "Me being from the House of Poison, you would think it was poison, right?"

"GIVE ME THE ANTIDOTE, NOW!" The lady screamed.

"Will you grant me passage? These are delicious, by the way."

"YES, I WILL GRANT YOU PASSAGE. THE ANTIDOTE! NOW!"

"Make her a nice cozy place to sleep and maybe draw a bath for her when she wakes up. It was just something to make her sleep for a moment. Trust me..." Pirouz raised his fist. "I've got needles in here that could've made it a lot worse." The woman could see the young girl resting peace-fully. "Honestly she's probably feeling great. Right now she is having dreams of pink clouds, most likely. She may feel a bit euphoric when she awakens." Pirouz stood up. "Care to share these with me?"

"I'm not hungry." The woman said, cranky that the little brat got one over her. Pirouz started to hear the first patters of the rain drops. He could tell it would soon start pouring.

"May I come in?"

She looked back at the kid. "Are you there?"

"Yes, grandma, let me sleep." The woman picked the kid up and walked deeper into the inn, saying as she did so: "Sit anywhere behind the counter." Pirouz complied.

Several minutes later, after the granddaughter's bed was made, Pirouz and the lady spoke over tea, as Pirouz had gorged himself on the dumplings. "I know what poison you used. You used Míngzé's poison. *Pink cloud.*"

"Yes, that is what I used. He said he knew you."

"Ha." She said, Pirouz could see a hint of a smile. "Míngzé only knows himself."

"What does that mean?"

"We became casual friends after I met him here. There was a woman who was in love with him, a friend of mine, also in the House of Poison, and he never noticed. It all ended tragically."

"How?" Pirouz asked, fascinated.

"Well how do you think things end tragically? She died. He never got to tell her how *he* felt, because it was quite clear he loved her too. Then she died, unexpectedly."

"How did she die?"

"A disease. I don't know what." She shrugged it all off. "Young man, life will give you plenty of these stories."

"Hm, master Míngzé never tells me anything about himself. None of the masters do."

"Foolish boy! Do you expect them to act out their lives for you?"

"No, I'm just saying, I don't know anything about them."

"I do, I know plenty. I can tell you about that group, I *do* have some stories."

"They're my shifus, so I don't know if I even want to hear them."

"I understand. Why are you here, boy?"

"Madame, I am afraid I cannot say." Stuffed with dumplings, Pirouz looked over her shoulder and noticed a tray holding a large bowl of candied fruits.

"If I gave you some candied fruit for your journey, would you tell me?" She asked.

"No, I can't. Technically, if I told you what I was doing here my shifus I think would kill me."

"Have some anyway." She took the bowl and placed it in front of Pirouz, his mouth was watering just from the sweet sticky smell of it all. He started picking through the bowl, singling out the sour cherries, which were his favorite. "You know, I can tell why many people come to Murder Mountain…”

"Oh? Please tell me."

"The Savior Sword."

"The *Savior Sword*? What's that?" He popped several more cherries into his mouth, savoring the sweetness.

"Let's just pretend I'm an idiot who doesn't think you know." She said.

"Okay." He replied, picking out a few more cherries, eating them one by one.

"There once lived a master killer who roamed the land, challenging everyone to mortal combat. They called him *Roaming Ghost.*"

"Roaming Ghost, huh? That sounds spooky." Pirouz.

"Spooky is an understatement. Legend says he killed more than ten thousand men and women in his journeys."

"Why was Roaming Ghost so disagreeable?" He asked.

"Why is *anyone* disagreeable? Life can be a pain sometimes."

"Yeah, I get that. Sometimes I want to kill ten thousand men too. Usually in the mornings." He said this, chewing the cherries. "But, what're you gonna do, am I right?"

"Roaming Ghost eventually fell in love."

"Eh, it happens."

"She demanded he kill the 7,000 evil men who were responsible for massacring her village and make a sword of their blood and kill the warlord who ordered the massacre with it."

"Wait, how do you make a sword of someone's blood? Was it frozen?"

"No, it was not frozen. You sure are awfully stupid!"

"I'm not stupid. I mean, how else would you kill someone with blood—unless it was diseased or something?"

"There are metals in the blood, boy. Iron. If you kill enough people, seven thousand to be exact, you will have enough iron to create a sword."

"Oh, that's interesting." He swallowed more cherries, acting like he hadn't heard of any of this. "I am mainly here to just take a nice long walk. Míngzé always says a nice long walk is good for the spirit, so I thought, hey, why not walk on Murder Mountain?"

"If that's true, you're either a fool or suicidal or both."

"I'm not suicidal," Pirouz said with a smile. He noticed footsteps from the front of the restaurant, shaking the floorboards. The footsteps sounded like they belonged to a two-ton animal. The entrance view was now blocked by a large, shadowy figure that looked like the shape of a mountain. Stepping in, the figure revealed itself to be a hulking giant of a man with a red face and angry eyes. He stepped through the place, causing little earthquakes with each step, then sat down at a table and slammed a large, sheathed saber on the table.

"Some wine, Auntie." Auntie threw a jug of wine at the rock of a man, who caught it with both hands, which looked like two large chunks of meat. He took a chug, then slammed the jug on the table. "Who's the boy?" He asked without looking at Pirouz.

"He's here for a walk." She said.

"No... he is here to die."

"Aren't we all?" Auntie replied. "Huang, if you are going to kill him, do it outside. I just cleaned up."

"Very well, I will kill the boy outside, after I have my wine."

"Hey, big man, I'm right here, talk to me directly."

"No, I refuse to." He grumbled, still not looking at him.

"You just did, though!" Pirouz shouted this while he pointed his finger at the mountain of a man. The man's face got even more sour than it naturally looked, he finally looked at Pirouz.

"I am going to make your death slow and painful by grinding all your bones together into a fine dust while it is all in your body. You will wish you were dead, and then I will take your body and throw it on the rocks near the water so the sharks can eventually eat you and the seagulls can pick at your bone paste." He took in another gulp of wine and looked at Pirouz. "I am Huang the Eyeball Squisher, and I will be crushing you soon. Know my name—so you can think about it while I destroy you."

"If you ever want to make fate laugh..." Pirouz threw one final candied cherry into the air and caught it with his mouth. "Just tell her your plans."

"What does that mean?" The giant's eyes were glowing with rage.

"That means..." Pirouz stood up, licked his sticky fingers clean, then rubbed them on his clothes. "Come at me, old man."

Huang stood up. "What is your name? I want to know the name of the little boy I am killing."

"I am Pirouz, son of King Yazdegerd, student of the House of Poison."

"*The House of Poison?*" Huang seemed pleasantly surprised by this. "I shall kill you with joy then."

Pirouz said nothing and simply lunged forward, unsheathing his blade only to be blocked by Huang, holding up his sheathed saber, blocking the blade, causing sparks to shoot out at Huang's face. Huang swung his saber down like a hammer, Pirouz did a back flip, dodging it just as the saber smashed through one of the tables, reducing it to sticks.

Auntie whistled, then screamed, "Outside! Huang! You owe me a table!"

Huang looked at Auntie. "Sorry, Auntie, I will make you a new one."

Just then, the little girl Pirouz had put to sleep was awake again, standing in the entranceway, rubbing her eyes. "Auntie, what's going on?"

"Just your typical mortal combat, dear. How are you feeling?"

"I feel very good." She rubbed her eyes and then went back into her room to sleep. Pirouz and Huang looked at one another, then went back to fighting. Pirouz swung his sword at Huang's face. Huang jerked his head back, missing the tip of the blade by a hair. Huang took both boulder-sized fists and, like a large primate, slammed them down on the floorboards, missing Pirouz, who leapt out of the way using his lightness kung fu, then stood by the door, sword out.

"Outside, big man, I don't want to ruin my new Auntie's establishment."

"Either way, you are dead."

"Eh, we're all dead or dying when you *think* about it."

Huang let out a fierce roar and ran towards Pirouz, who simply bolted out of the restaurant and back to the grassy field outside. The inn rumbled as Huang stomped outside like a rhino. "Prepare to be crushed!"

"Okay." Pirouz closed his eyes, sarcastically, then opened them. "I'm prepared! Come at me, fat boy!" Pirouz unsheathed his sword.

"You will eat your words—I'll make sure of it!"

For some reason, this irritated Pirouz. "You know what?" Pirouz took a few steps forward. "Maybe the long boat ride has me feeling a little annoyed. I'm in the mood to beat you with my bare hands."

"Hahahahah!" Huang laughed. "Silly, silly boy! Beat *me*?! I am Huang, the feared keeper of the peace here on Blood Orange Island!"

"You? But how? You're so chunky!" Pirouz said this with a chuckle.

"I am the official constable of the island! I am the one who makes sure garbage like you doesn't make it past the great waterfalls."

"Hm. Interesting. So the island has a jail?"

"Of sorts. You will see it, soon enough. You will be tortured for the rest of your days."

"Gee, I don't like the sound of that. Come here for your ass-whooping." Pirouz got into his fighting stance and winked. The wink made Constable Huang furious. With a tiger like roar, he jumped into the air to deliver a flying kick toward Pirouz's face, which Pirouz dodged smoothly, ramming Huang's body into the closest tree, smashing it into splinters. Huang landed on his back. As he reached for the saber, Pirouz did a flip in the air, then landed with his feet on Huang's chest, knocking the air out of his lungs. Huang burst up, making Pirouz fly back. He landed softly on his feet, using his lightness kung fu. Huang got up, his eyes were practically red with anger. His girth did not stop him from moving quickly, in a flash, he was in front of Pirouz, saber raised high, bringing it down like a boulder crashing down a hill. Pirouz unsheathed his sword and split the saber in half on impact. Huang held both pieces and looked at them, shocked. Pirouz sliced his blade down the length of Huang's robe, ripping it soundlessly. He sheathed his sword so he could deliver two dozen firecracker-fast punches to Huang's chest, knocking the wind clean out of him. Pirouz delivered the final punch, blasting Huang off his feet and onto his back. He gasped for air on the ground.

Auntie, by this point had watched the whole thing unfold by the entrance of the restaurant. She stepped out as Pirouz walked over to Huang's squirming body. Pirouz looked down at Huang. He wanted to punch his face into a fine pulp. He flipped Huang on his stomach, who was too busy struggling to breathe to fight Pirouz. Pirouz reached down and ripped the back of Huang's robe, revealing his large, scarred up back.

"What'd you do that for?" Auntie asked.

"Because..." Pirouz landed a chop to the back of Huang's head, knocking him into a deep sleep. "I was checking to see if he had a tattoo of a hummingbird and a dragon."

"Why?" Auntie asked.

"Because the person who killed Master Míngzé had a tattoo like that."

"Míngzé was killed?"

"Yes, and his killer is on the island, it's the reason I am here... to find him."

A flood of memories washed through Pirouz's mind as he stood up. He remembered that after Míngzé was killed, he saw a traveling show in the local town square to cheer himself up. He fell in love with the contortionist, a young lady of impossible beauty who called herself Crystal Sparrow. After the show the performers put on where she danced and twisted herself into impossible shapes, Pirouz went to a tavern where she was drinking. She approached him—much to his surprise—and the two spoke of life, art, and death. She was so tired from drinking and performing that she had him carry her to her troop's wagon, and she kissed him. When the wagon left, he noticed she had dropped a scarf that was draped around her neck, which had a crystal sparrow embroidered on it. He vowed to return it to her—*if* he survived Murder Mountain.

He knew, however, that the chances of that were slim, as his adversaries would only get more deadly as he traveled upwards, and if he dared return from the island without the Savior Sword... the House of Poison would surely kill him, despite him being one of their pupils.

It was just the way it was... to fail meant to be killed, either quickly or slowly, it did not matter. He was determined to find the sword and see the young lady he loved once more and return her scarf. He also had to discover who Míngzé's killer was, even if it killed him. *I'm pretty much a dead man walking,* Pirouz thought. *I have to keep going, but I can feel death waiting for me.*

Chapter 2:
Blood of the Past

Snow was falling on the House of Poison.

Jiao Long, one of Pirouz's five shifus, stood before him, showing off the new sword they had just taken from a local warlord earlier in the week. Pirouz had never seen such a beautiful blade. "It's a pity we must return this." Jiao Long swung the sword around a few more times just to feel it again. It was the lightest blade he had ever held. "You and Míngzé will give it to the emperor."

"Shifu, with respect, I'm perfecting my Eagle style this evening with Master Zhang Li."

"She will understand, and you have your entire life to perfect each style, young student. We need you to accompany him for very simple reasons, Pirouz." Jiao Long moved into the dojo and Pirouz followed. "You *are* the emperor's brother-in-law, technically speaking." Jiao Long was now in the kitchen, pouring himself some tea Master Míngzé had brewed earlier that morning. "While I would love to devote our time solely to the advancement of our martial skills, unfortunately, politics is always something to be considered." He took a sip of his tea then gazed off into nothing, looking lost in melancholy. "The House of Poison *must* be in the emperor's good graces at all times, otherwise, we are just killers- gangsters. Mercenaries. Under the auspices of the emperor, we are patriots." He took another sip of his tea. Pirouz could sense a deep feeling of sadness in Jiao Long's eyes. "Tell Zhang Li of the change of plans."

Pirouz left the kitchen and walked to the garden on the other side of the dojo. Zhang Li was sitting quietly beneath a cherry blossom tree. He saw her deep in meditation and turned to leave—when she suddenly spoke, stopping him. "Are you going with Míngzé to give the blade to the emperor?"

she asked..

"Yes, I apologize for the change of plans, master."

"I knew that would happen. Our lessons can resume tomorrow. Leave me be."

Pirouz bowed. "Yes, Master." Pirouz left the garden and was heading up to his quarters when Cong stopped him with his trademark smile.

"You're gonna go see your brother-in-law?" He asked.

"Yeah." Pirouz couldn't help but smile, knowing Cong had some sort of joke ready to go.

"Are you gonna ask for a pardon for the guy we took the sword from?" Cong said with a giggle.

Pirouz let out a laugh, remembering the war lord begging them for a pardon from the emperor before they took the sword. "I will. Even though he is headless, I will honor his wishes and ask for a pardon."

"When are you leaving?" Cong asked.

"Morning." Pirouz said. He turned when he heard the footsteps of Yuze lumbering into the garden after his day of hunting, holding a large boar over his head with a big smile. He slammed the boar onto the ground before Zhang Li, Cong, and Pirouz.

"Whoa, that's the size of a horse," Cong said.

"Yeah, I saw this beast last week and made a note to hunt her down. Pirouz, do you want to help me butcher it?"

"I would, but I have to prepare for my trip tomorrow, Míngzé and I are seeing the emperor."

"Oh, that sounds fun. At any rate, come with me as I prepare to carve it up. I'm sure you can spare a minute."

Pirouz followed Yuze to the kitchen. He slapped the boar onto the large slab where Yuze usually cut up what he had hunted. Pirouz looked the boar in its dead eye, then looked at its stomach, where four arrows were sticking out. "She was a fearsome one." Yuze pulled a knife off the rack and stabbed it into the pig's belly. Its intestines spilled out as he carved up the length of the pig's stomach. "Life is miraculous, isn't it, Pirouz? This beast that I hunted down had an essence, an energy, some would describe this energy as *beautiful.* I just think it is what it is. In order for us to survive on some level, we must destroy the creature's essence, like one would vanquish the flame of a candle by pressing your fingers against it."

"Yes. this makes me hungry," Pirouz said, backing away as the pig's guts spilled out.

"Same." He put the knife down. "Pirouz, it is very important -for us- that you always stay in the good graces of the emperor."

"Yeah, of course. Everyone tells me. Why wouldn't I? He calls me his son."

"Yes, this is true. Always remember that because of that, you could have lived an easier life. You could have stayed with the emperor and your sister and lived in the lap of luxury. Instead, you decided to live and be trained by *us.* Even under the emperor, you go by the same rules as we do... rules that, if broken, can lead to your death. Know that you chose this."

"Yes master, I did..." Pirouz looked away from the pig to Master Yuze. "I don't want the royal life, I want the life of a martial hero, it makes more sense." The walls of the House of Poison shook with a loud boom, like a hundred fireworks going off at once.

"The courtyard, go!" Using his lightness kung fu, Pirouz leapt out the window, landing on the branch of the large tree that stood between the kitchen and the courtyard. Pirouz twirled through the air, brushing over the bushes and landing on his feet to see master Míngzé standing before a cloud of smoke, ready to fight whatever was there when the smoke cleared.

"Pirouz, stand back," Míngzé said as the smoke drifted past him, revealing a figure clad in black and gold with a mask on. From the build, it appeared to be a man. He put his fists up.

"Míngzé ... the day of your death is today." The voice was so deep and raspy it sounded like it belonged to a demon.

"I don't think so, coward." The two soared toward each

other, trading blows midair, then landed on their feet only to trade more blows. The assassin was skilled, as each blow was expertly blocked and countered. Pirouz could tell the moves were from someone who had trained in Míngzé's style. Míngzé landed a blow directly across the assassin's face, knocking him to the right. Pirouz felt his heart leap with joy, witnessing his master land a solid blow, knocking the would-be killer to his side. The assassin pumped both fists, revealing two large blades that slid out of the tops of his hands, making him seem like a wild beast with swords for appendages. He slid the blades across from each other, causing a spark to travel down the length of the swords and zap out of the tip, hitting Míngzé in the chest, causing him to fall back but still land on his feet. Míngzé shot a poisonous dart at the villain, who dodged it as the dart landed squarely in front of Pirouz's eyes, slamming itself into a wooden column.

Just as Zhang Li and Cong breezed into the court yard from the roof, the assassin jumped over Míngzé's body and brought his blades down, stabbing him in the heart. He ripped the blades out, a gushing of bright red blood sprayed out of Míngzé's chest, splashing over the snowy stone ground, painting the ice in a deep crimson. In his last moment, Míngzé stabbed at the assailant's back with a hidden blade, it tore the fabric of the murderer's black clothing, revealing a tattoo of a hummingbird and a dragon. "MASTER!" Pirouz shouted. He ran at the killer, but before he could reach him, the killer leapt backwards, up and over the courtyard wall, out of sight. Pirouz followed him, dashing into the woods, leaping over the tree branches using the very methods taught to him by Míngzé. He could see this person had the Savior Sword. He heard the sound of Cong calling for him when he noticed this:

"Pirouz, return! Now!" Pirouz stopped, knowing better than to defy his master, and turned back to the House of Poison courtyard. Zhang Li and Cong stood over Míngzé's body. The freezing cold caused his blood to form a red mist floating around him. Pirouz looked down at his now-dead master in complete shock.

Yuze ran into the yard, now wearing his blue leaopard armor, with two swords out. "Who dares challenge the House of Poison?!" Yuze stopped at the sight of Master Míngzé's body on the ground. "Míngzé!"

"I know that smoke," Cong said.

"Yes, whoever did this is long gone. I too know these tactics," Zhang Li said.

"Why can't we go find them? They're not long gone!"

"Don't question her, boy," Yuze said. "That smoke..." Yuze seemed spooked. "The last time we saw that smoke..."

"Was on Murder Mountain," Zhang Li said. Jiao Long leapt into the courtyard from the wall. Zhang Li shouted at him, sharply: "Where were *you*?"

"I was out walking. What has happened?" As he looked down at Míngzé's body.

Cong said coldly, "Isn't it obvious? Someone has killed Mingzé and taken the Savior Sword.

The image of Míngzé in a pool of his own blood, surrounded by the white of the falling snow, was on Pirouz's mind as Auntie packed him some dumplings for the road. She warned him: "This is nothing."

"What is nothing?" Pirouz said, taking a bite of one of the dumplings. He noticed Huang outside, getting up, seemingly meditating on his defeat.

"Him, he is nothing. He's just an oaf. You have not even begun to walk up the mountain."

"Well, I did pretty well, no?"

"You may have House of Poison training, and you may be able to fight through many men, but once a blade slices your throat or a fist smashes your insides into mush, none of that matters, boy."

"Regardless, I need my revenge." Pirouz stepped out of the inn and gave Huang a smart-aleck nod and smile.

"Revenge is good sometimes, but other times it can feel empty."

"Here's to hoping that's not the case. *I* personally think that the type of revenge I am getting will be good for my health." Pirouz stopped walking, remembering to ask, "So, tell me about the three monks."

"Like you don't know?" Auntie joined Pirouz, both of them standing in the grass. "I am sure if you have heard of them, you have heard all you need to know."

"I need to hear it from someone who's basically their neighbor. You follow?"

"I suggest you stay in the spare room for the night. If you face them at nightfall, you will undoubtedly die. If you face them in the sunrise, you may have a fighting chance." Pirouz was in no rush, this sounded like a good idea. Over tea, Auntie explained: "The three monks were three friends who lived in a fishing town. The legend goes that bandits wiped out their village and since then, they devoted themselves to mastering the martial arts. They tracked down the bandits and killed them just seven years after the massacre."

"That is a very heartwarming story. You don't suppose they would just let me slip by?"

"They are devoted to protecting the Savior Sord. There is no possible way they will let you pass."

"Okay, so let's say I try to sneak up one side, they'll catch me?"

"The people who inhabit this island tend to be very sharp, young man. Chances are, everyone knows you're here." When she said this, Pirouz imagined every warrior he'd heard of on the mountain — those spoken of by his masters, and those from nightmares. "Let me show you your room." Pirouz was led to a small room where Auntie pickled various things like cabbage and garlic and other vegetables that could be pickled. "If you break any of these — especially those," she said, pointing to several jars placed on cupboards high above the rest, "I will be very irritated. Trust me, you don't want to see that."

"You weren't irritated before?"

"From *you*?" She scoffed. "You think too highly of yourself, young man." She left the room. Pirouz placed his sword and bag down and sat in the center of the room to meditate.

After doing so, he looked at his map. *If the woman likes some-one, she will let them stay with her. It is safe in her little inn.* He remembered Míngzé saying this once, when describing the mountain. He had looked at the map countless times, but only now did he appreciate the various points designated for rest. The day's events were nowhere near as intense as others Pirouz had witnessed in his lifetime — yet he was exhausted. He lay down in the middle of the room and closed his eyes.

He dreamed of his father's murder, which he had wit-nessed as a small boy. Pirouz often had flashes of violence that jolted him awake, but this memory was the one he hated most. His dream replayed blood pouring down his father's neck from another man's knife. He gasped and awoke. A man in a mask was standing before him. It was... the man who killed Míngzé. Pirouz shot to his feet. The masked figure struck several of his pressure points in less than a millisec-ond, paralyzing him on the spot.

"You are not welcome here... boy. You are not welcome anywhere."

Pirouz, through gritted teeth, snarled: "You killed my master and I will destroy you for it."

"You are in no position to destroy anything, boy. You are but a flea — not even worth dealing with. I'm here to tell you to leave. If you don't, I'll kill the remaining members of the House of Poison... and leave you alive to witness the carnage — before I murder you."

"You can kill one of us in the shadows because you're a coward, but you'll never face down the House of Poison. My masters will kill you a million times over before you hit the ground for murdering Master Míngzé."

"So tell me boy - why haven't they done this already?" Pir-ouz didn't respond. He simply stewed in his anger, unable to move. "I've killed mothers in front of their children — and fa-thers the same way. I've even killed children in front of their parents. I enjoy taking things from others... but my favorite thing to take... is a life they hold precious." If you further an-ger me by staying on the island... I will be sure to take every life you know." He raised his fist and slammed a glass capsule to the ground, which caused a purple cloud of smoke to burst with a loud bang. Auntie burst into the room a few moments later, not seeing Pirouz through the smoke, she knocked him over. He hit the wall, causing it to shake and knock a jar of pickled garlic to the floor, cracking the lid off. Auntie pulled Pirouz to his feet and struck several pressure points with her middle finger, freeing his muscle constriction and allowing him to move again.

"I must leave," Pirouz said, cracking his neck.

"I think that's a good idea." She looked at the lid of the pickled garlic jar—it was cracked in two, but the jar itself, miraculously, hadn't broken. "Take the garlic."

"I'm sorry about that."

"I don't care... I care more about the fact that *he* just came here."

"Who is *he*?"

"He is the Master Killer." She took an empty jar from the corner of the room and poured the pickled garlic into it. "He first arrived on the island about a year ago."

"That's when my master was killed."

"That makes sense then." She shook her head. "The first thing he did was kill the Green Wolf Clan."

"How many of them did he kill?"

"Most of them." She handed Pirouz the jar of pickled garlic.

"That's insane." Pirouz said, admitting to himself that it scared him. "My masters used to say a member of the Green Wolf Clan was nearly impossible to kill." Pirouz walked out of the pickling room. Auntie followed.

"He proved them wrong. He challenged the entire clan to a death match and murdered them all in less than ten minutes—or so I've been told."

"Who told you this?"

"I did." The young girl—Auntie's assistant—was up, awakened by the boom in the night. "He killed my family."

"You were in the Green Wolf Clan?"

"Yes..." The child said. "Please kill him for me."

Pirouz gave a solemn nod, thanked Auntie for her eventual hospitality and the pickled garlic, then moved on his way, holding his sheathed blade tightly. Pirouz reached the path leading up to what were called the blood falls. He stopped. He could hear the raging waters just beyond the trees, over the hill. He took in a deep breath. Any fear he had was ignored. He proceeded to walk up the path, gripping the handle of his blade even tighter. The waterfalls were lit by thousands of fireflies, which hovered over the lake, just below the large rock mountain from which the great waters poured. Pirouz stopped. He saw, as though they were hovering above the waters, the Three Monks—sitting in deep meditation with their eyes closed. The three men were bald and wore simple robes, one orange, one blue, and one green. The one in the middle opened his eyes.

"You are welcome to join us in mediation." He said. Pirouz simply gave this a nod and sat on a rock right before the lake of water. He closed his eyes and pretended to meditate with them. He was too nervous to feel zen. Instead, he hoped in joining the men, they would let him pass. This wish was destroyed when he heard the man in the middle say:

"Do not think that because we let you meditate with us, we will let you pass." Pirouz opened his eyes. Each monk now stood on a different side of the lake. The green-robed man in the middle stood on the highest rock, looking down at Pirouz. "We know why you are here..."

The blue-robed monk dashed into the air and landed on the water, barely causing a ripple, before springing back up, flipping around and landing on the path from where Pirouz arrived. "It is too late for you to turn back. You must face your death." He said.

"Yeah!" The orange-robed monk shouted.

"Sirs, is there truly no way you'll let me pass in peace?"

"Absolutely not, young man. It is just the way it is." Green Robe slid on the water like it was ice and softly glided towards Pirouz, landing just a few feet away from him. "You'll be crushed like all the others—no more, no less."

"Very well then." Pirouz sighed and got into his fighting stance just as the monk reached out to strike him with a tiger claw attack which Pirouz dodged and countered with a high kick to the monk's face. The monk blocked it, seized Pirouz's leg, and hurled him across the lake as the fireflies parted from his path. He hit the rocks across the water. The blue-robed monk did a flip and landed on the rock in front of Pirouz. Pirouz got to his feet. The Blue Monk lunged at him, and the two exchanged a lightning-fast flurry of strikes, each blocked or deflected in perfect rhythm. The Blue Monk traded one last blow, then did a back flip across the water to the branch of a tree hanging over the lake. "You are well trained." He said.

"Yeah, thanks for the observation." Pirouz said this, then shifted his attention to the orange-robed monk who skated across the water to deliver a powerful punch to Pirouz's chest before he could react. Pirouz flew back first towards the waterfall, splashing through, skidding across the surface of the cave just behind the falls. He thrusted himself back to his feet. "Alright, monks. If we're gonna do this, let's *really* do this and not waste any time." He unsheathed his blade. "COME AT ME! AT THE SAME DAMN TIME, LIKE YOU WANNA KILL ME YOU BASTARDS!" He heard the blades of the monks slide out of their sheathes and could see the flash of them fly towards him from behind the water.

The three monks leaped into the cave, Pirouz deflected each strike, sparks flying wildly as he spun like a whirlwind. The monks backed off, spooked.

"Where did you learn that, young man?" The green-robed monk asked.

"What's it to *you?*" Pirouz said quickly, backing away towards the falling water.

"Are you a disciple of Míngzé?" The orange-robed monk asked this with reverence in his voice.

"Yes." Pirouz raised his sword. "I am here to find the bastards that killed him."

"Míngzé is dead?" The blue-robed monk asked.

"Yeah—hence why I'm hunting the man who killed him. So either let me pass so I can go about my retribution or *die*."

The monks all laughed. "Quite funny, boy, to hear a student of Míngzé speak so aggressively. "Míngzé was a sweet man—but some of his students were downright vicious!" The green-robe said.

Blue-robe snorted: "He was *not* a sweet man. I'm glad he's dead."

Orange-robe looked shocked: "Don't say such a thing!"

The green-robe interjected with a smile: "Young man, you must understand, we all knew Míngzé when he trained in Shao-Lin. We were friends."

"Speak for yourself, he was no friend of mine." Blue-robe looked like he was hiding a painful story.

"Yes, this one did not like Míngzé; they fought and Míngzé defeated him quite quickly."

"Hogwash! I was ill that day!" Blue-robe shouted this like a petulant child.

"Who killed Míngzé?" The orange-robe asked.

"It was a man in a mask. A true coward. He is on the island. I am here to kill him and take the Savior Sword. If you do not let me pass, we must resume our death match."

"I have no problem with that... boy." Blue-robe pointed his sword at Pirouz. Pirouz raised his sword in a snap, making the two points touch and spark right at the tip.

"We have been tasked with protecting the entrance to the mountain." Green-robe said. "What you do beyond our area of the mountain is of no concern to me, whatever the world allows, it allows."

"I must also say..." Green-robe continued. "That Míngzé was a friend to *us*, he was a good man, and we wish you good fortune on your path to finding the killer."

"And since we *were* like brothers to Míngzé, him and I will let you pass." Orange-robe then looked at Blue Robe, standing there with his sword up and a mean look on his face. "*He* however despised Míngzé and anybody associated with him. So I believe he will be trying to kill you with all of his might.

"That is very bad I suppose," Pirouz said.

"Who is to say what is good or bad?" The blue-robed monk asked. The two raised their swords and clanged them across one another. Pirouz hit him with a hurricane attack, clashing his sword against the monk's like a metal razored wood pecker.

"He is quite skilled." The blue-robed monk whispered to the orange, though Pirouz could not hear, for his entire body and frame of mind had gone into berserker mode. The Blue-robed monk blocked a sideswipe from Pirouz, causing Pirouz's sword to crack against the cave rocks, sending a painful vibration through his hand. He dropped his sword but caught it midair with the other hand, kicking the attacking monk in the face in the process. Pirouz jumped out of the cave and slid back-first across the water, hitting a large boulder at the center of the lake. He pumped his fist, cracking his knuckles. He waited for the monk to come out of the cave, then realized it had been far too long. The windy sound of fabric fluttering in the air flew at him, and he looked up to see the Blue Monk jumping down on him from the top of the waterfall.

Pirouz and the Blue Monk clashed swords once more, causing the fireflies to scatter in the air with the light streaming behind them. Blue Monk found an opening just as Pirouz missed a chance to bring the blade down on the monk's shoulder. The Blue Monk's sword swiped across Pirouz's face, who stepped and leaned back enough for the blade to simply slice the skin on the bridge of his nose. Pirouz leaped back, jumped off of the surface of the water, and did a back flip back onto the mainland of the mountain. The Blue Monk followed him with his sword out, mimicking his bounce off the water. "Do you know why I hated Míngzé?" He asked.

"No, I am sure it was jealousy."

"Ha! What does he have that I should be jealous of! He doesn't even have hair!" The monk said with roaring laughter.

"He has hair." Pirouz smiled in such a way that it made the monk furious.

"BOY! DO YOU NOT KNOW WHO YOU SPEAK TO!?!?!" The Blue Monk's face was turning redder than a radish.

"Yes, bald Blue Monk."

"SILENCE!" he shouted.

"Nah," Pirouz said. The Blue Monk charged towards Pirouz, growling with anger. Pirouz counterattacked him with four swipes of the blade, then tricked him into making a big swing. Pirouz moved his head aside, causing Blue's blade to hit a boulder behind him, causing his sword to shatter.

"Impossible!" The blue said, looking at his shattered blade.

"Nothing is," Pirouz said. "I'll make it fair." Pirouz sheathed his sword and landed a lightning flurry of punches to the monk's chest. The final punch caused Blue Monk to fall flat on his back, wincing in pain. The other two monks leapt into the air, across the lake, and landed softly at their fellow monk's feet.

"Perhaps the universe is telling you to put aside your grudge against Míngzé, brother. The man is dead now and there are far worse people in the world and on the mountain than this young man seeking vengeance." Orange Monk said this solemnly, then looked at Pirouz and pursed his lips, nodding. "He has unresolved anger towards your late master."

Blue Monk snarled at this, then jumped up into an upright position. He pointed at Pirouz. "I will get you, boy, just not now."

"Don't you point at me, boy." Pirouz said this with a smile beneath his serious face. The other two monks laughed.

"Oh goodness! He called you a *boy*." Orange Monk was doubled over in laughter. Green Monk was in a fit of giggles himself. "Will you be making a detailed plan for your retaliation?" The Orange Monk laughed.

"If he is, should I just... hang out until he's ready. Take your time, by the way." Pirouz sat on a boulder. "I'll be here I guess, with my new friends."

"I like this one." Green Robe said, containing his laughter. "Tell me, young man, how did you come to train in the

House of Poison? They are known in the martial world not to be very welcoming."

"All jokes aside, is this guy gonna wait till I'm not looking and—" Pirouz made a throat-slitting gesture.

"Noooo." Orange Robe said with a groan. "He will be quite over it." He looked at Blue Robe. "Aren't you over it already?" He asked.

"Absolutely not, I will not entertain this cretin." Blue Robe jumped across the lake and into the cave, disappearing.

"He will sulk, then meditate, then sleep, then calm down. You do not worry, young man." Orange said with a nod of the head. The two monks sat on boulders across from Pirouz. "I say, though, young man, it is quite curious that such a young person would be as skilled as you are, let alone getting to this point of the mountain."

"I don't if I'm too far. Do people usually make it this far?" Pirouz asked, hoping for an ego-boosting answer.

"Some do, but many do not even make it past the shore." The blue-robed monk said. "The worst was when it was first known that the Savior Sword was here. Many masters of the martial arts, and many not-so-skilled, arrived on the shores."

"What happened?" Pirouz asked.

"What do you think happened? It was an absolute blood-bath." Orange Robe said with weary eyes.

"Master Míngzé *did* say something to the effect of many masters fighting each other when the sword arrived, but never in detail."

"It was a gory sight indeed. The ocean ran red with blood. All in all, in one day, thirty-some-odd martial masters were pulverized, crushed, cut, bled, and died, in a very short amount of time."

"We buried the bodies up in the cemetery, just a little bit away from here."

"That must be one interesting cemetery."

"Yes, we advise you to stay away from it the best you can. The Blood Sucker lives there."

"The *Blood Sucker*?" Pirouz asked.

"Yes he is one of the more fearsome people, or should I say creatures-on the island."

"Why is he called *The Blood Sucker?*"

"Because he *sucks blood!*" The Orange Monk shouted this, sounding scared.

"Is he a man?" Pirouz asked.

"Yes, he looks like one, though a demented one."

"Ah," Pirouz said.

"Do not be flippant of the Blood Sucker, he has powers beyond any of us. He can transform into a beast for goodness' sake!"

"Is he nice?" Pirouz asked, innocently enough.

"Nice?! The creature drinks blood! How can he be *nice!?!* Despite your obvious training, you are a very silly young man!"

"I don't want problems with someone if I don't need to."

"If that is the case, know that the cemetery is easily avoidable."

"Yeah, my map goes around it. My masters warned me not to go to the cemetery. That it was a dead zone."

"Of course they did! That is where the Blood Sucker lives!"

"Anything else about the mountain I need to know?"

"Just avoid the Blood Sucker, at all costs."

"Aside from that."

"Did auntie give you candied fruit?" Orange Monk asked, sounding like a gluttonous child.

"Yeah, you want some?" Pirouz asked, not wanting to give him any but knowing that in the end, generosity with a new friend was not a bad thing.

"Could I?" He asked.

"Of course, new friend. Would you like some too?" Pirouz asked the Green Robe.

"I am okay, thank you, you must conserve your food." He looked at Orange Monk.

"Don't take the candied fruit. He needs it."

"I am sorry, I just love it so much."

"Don't take it, you boar!"

"Me, a boar? The universe brought candied berries our way. I am not going to pass that up!"

"The boy needs his food!" The Green Monk growled.

"Oh but be serious... he will surely die!"

"That may be, but he can at least die with a full stomach!"

"Wait, guys, why do you say I will surely die? I took the three of you on."

"Yes, young man, that is respectable, but in all actuality, you will die. That is why we are letting you pass. If we honestly believed you would go up the mountain and walk into the temple and take the Savior Sword, we would kill you where you stand. The truth is, however, you make us laugh and smile and we like that you made a baby out of our friend over there."

"Gentlemen, that hurts."

"Sorry." Green Robe said.

"It's okay." Pirouz said. He got up.

"Where are you going?" Orange Robe asked.

"Up the mountain, obviously. To die, I guess like you said."

"Have you even slept?" The green-robed monk asked, sounding like a concerned uncle.

"Honestly? Not really."

"I think if you are going to die you should have a full belly and be well rested." He got up to his feet and extended his arm. "Please, follow me."

The temple the monks lived in was just above the falls. The sun was rising as they climbed the steps leading up to it. Pirouz was so tired he was dragging his hand across the mossy rocks as he walked for support. It was a modest temple from the outside, looking like it was carved out of the side of the mountain. Stepping inside, Pirouz was overwhelmed by how big it looked, with a ceiling that stretched high above and a pathway to an altar streaming with incense.

"I always thought there was a chance Míngzé would join us one day." Orange Robe said as Blue Robe and Green Robe went off to their living quarters. "I am afraid I did not ask your name, do you mind telling me?"

"I am Pirouz."

The monk stopped. "You are the son of Yazdegerd." He said.

There was a pause.

The monk looked at Pirouz. "I know you." The monk's friendly face was now one of serious empathy. "I am Bo. The one you fought was Bai. Our other brother is Bingwen... we brought you to safety... when you were young. You may not remember."

"I try not to." Pirouz said.

The monk gave Pirouz a blanket and let him sleep in the cave outside the temple, the bigger one near the top of the falls. Pirouz had a candle burning, he was looking at the map. Bo, Bai and Bingwen left him alone to sleep. He knew it would be hard, but he needed to conserve his energy if he was going to survive this experience, and he knew that he had already felt like he had climbed *twenty* mountains.

As he closed his eyes, he could not help but think of his father, and what had happened when he was just a boy.

The thoughts turned into a dream.

Several years prior, when Pirouz was just five winters old, Pirouz stood frozen as the blood sprayed out of his father Yazdegerd's throat. The man behind him had welcomed them onto his property just several days before. He then waited for the perfect chance to hold Yazdegerd's face with one hand, while he carved the knife further across his throat with the other. Pirouz was completely still, as the man gave no warning he was going to do what he was doing. The geyser of blood stained the wood on the floor and steadily died down in a rhythmic pump as Yazdegerd's heart stopped. He looked at his son and tried to say something, but his blood clogged throat could only muster up a gargle before he dropped to his knees, then fell to his side.

King Yazdegerd was dead.

Pirouz looked at his father, on the floor. His eyes were wide open, but it was clear to Pirouz that he was dead. Pirouz looked at the man, who smiled.

"Royal affairs are a messy business," he said, wiping the knife. "Of which I know nothing about." He looked at Pirouz with a somewhat sympathetic look in his eyes. "My boy, I am just a poor grain miller." Pirouz did not understand why the man was telling him this, all he could see was the sight of his father, dead on the floor. "Life is a struggle, you know, and this was an opportunity... I have a family- I know you don't understand." The man stopped wiping the blade. He held it up to the shaft of light that beamed through the entrance of the grain miller's place of business, a flash hit Pirouz's eye from the blade's reflection. "He wanted me to kill you, too." He pointed the knife at Pirouz. "My boy... I want you to come here."

"Why?" Pirouz asked, hoping he wouldn't say what he was going to say.

"So I can finish the job." The man smiled. "I will make sure to do it fast." Pirouz pulled out the dagger his father had given him. He hissed, like a snake and swiped the knife towards the miller, whose smile got even warmer in response. "Don't make this difficult, little one. Children die every day. It's nothing to feel bad about." Pirouz threw the dagger at the man, the handle hit him in the forehead. A lump swelled up on the man's skull, the red tip turned into a river of blood that streamed down his face in a single red line. "You little idiot!" The miller slapped his hand over his head. Pirouz used this as an opportunity to run right between the entrance and the miller, who tried but failed to grab him as he passed.

The sun was bright, it gave the field of wheat an orange glow. Pirouz ran towards the field, hoping to lose the miller as the wheat went well above Pirouz's head. He could hear the miller behind him, ripping the fabric of the entrance as he ran outside, muttering curse words. Pirouz trampled over the crops as he ran, jumping to his left and making another path in an effort to lose the miller... which did not do much good.

The miller followed the trail until he could see the boy running and crushing the wheat under his leather sandals. *Those sandals will make a good gift for my nephew, his entire outfit would, in fact,* the miller thought. Pirouz could sense the miller was quickly approaching; he could hear his grunting breaths getting closer, sounding like a ravenous pig the closer he got. Pirouz wondered frantically how long the wheat field would last. Pirouz could hear a break in the man's running, followed by a crash behind him as he made a failed attempt to tackle the boy. Pirouz looked behind him, then, before he could get a full view of the miller on the ground, two large, callused hands grabbed hold of him and lifted him up.

"Break his neck!" The miller cried to the man holding Pirouz. It was the miller's brother, who introduced himself to Pirouz and Yazdegerd when they sought refuge on their property just several days prior.

"We can sell him," the miller's brother said, holding his hand tightly over Pirouz's mouth. He was already imagining what kind of trade the boy might fetch.

"No, kill him. The little bastard made me bleed."

Suddenly, Pirouz saw a piece of metal fly toward him. The man who was holding him suddenly released his grip when Pirouz could hear the sound of the metal piercing itself through his attacker. It was an arrow. The man released him and collapsed, blood spurting from his neck where the arrow stood straight up. The miller's eyes darted around the field, and he swung the knife around in a paranoid frenzy. Another flash of metal soundlessly flowed towards the miller, hitting him in the chest. He fell flat on his back, dead. Pirouz looked at the bodies. The wheat rustled. A large shadow fell over Pirouz.

"You must come with me now." The man had a thick, black beard and had the physique of a bear. A bow was slung over his shoulder, and he carried a sword with an unusually curved blade. Pirouz took several steps back, then darted away from the man. His father told him that should something happen to him, the price on his head would be high, and thus, Pirouz should trust no one should he find himself alone. So he ran through the wheat fields. He was afraid to look behind him, but he could hear the clanking of the man's armor as he ran after him. The clanking getting louder with each frenzied moment. Pirouz cut a right, deeper into the field, hoping the sudden change in direction would throw off his pursuer. It did not, as the sound of his rustling armor only got louder.

He kept running to where the field ended, he saw his father's body where he was killed, lying face up near a tree outside the miller's home, he realized he had run in a circle. He ran towards his father's body to retrieve the dagger he kept on him. He caught a glimpse of the man behind him, who looked agitated at all the running. Pirouz leapt forward towards his father's body to get the dagger, he pulled it out of its sheath, then turned to face his would-be killer. Just as he raised the blade toward the man, an arrow ripped through his sleeve and nailed it to a tree behind him. His hand held onto the knife, he grabbed it with the other hand and swung it at the man, whose golden armor shone so bright it made Pirouz squint.

"I mean you no harm, Pirouz. I was instructed by your father to take you to safety."

"Father said I can't trust anyone."

"He was right... you can't." The man stepped closer, it was clear, now that Pirouz could see him closer, that he was (or once was) a soldier of high rank. "But in my case trusting me is what is going to help you survive." The man crouched down, so he was eye level with the boy. "Everyone wants to kill you now, Pirouz. If you don't come with me you won't survive. It's very simple." He stepped closer to him. "I am going to release you, don't run. If I wanted to kill you you'd already be dead." He plucked the arrow out of the tree. Pirouz shook his arm, then looked at his father with a blank look on his face. "We don't have time, come, let's go." Pirouz kept staring back at his father's body as the man lead him to the other side of the miller's property, where a saddled horse was waiting. The man helped Pirouz up, then climbed aboard himself after untying the horse from the tree it was strapped to.

"The journey will be long, Pirouz."

"Where are we going?"

"Somewhere far away, and safe. My name is Azman." They rode to an inn a short way away from the miller's property. Pirouz rode behind Azman in silence, his eyes fixed on the brown spots on the horse's back. Azman hitched the horse to a trough and ordered Pirouz to follow him into the inn after helping him down from the horse.

"*Osh*." Azman said to the innkeeper, an old man who looked to be recovering from a nap. The osh was served. "Eat."

"I'm not hungry."

"We have a long journey ahead of us."

"Where are we going?"

"Far." Azman slurped his soup. "Everyone wants to kill you." Azman's attention went to the entrance, a slender man with a sword slung sheathed under his arm was walking in, he looked at Azman and Pirouz, stopped, and smirked. Azman simply turned back around. He slurped the osh from his bowl, the slender man sat down next to him. Azman now sat between the boy and the thin man. He grumbled, under his breath so the innkeeper couldn't hear: "Your scroll,"

"You're just going to get right into business?"

"Yes, show me."

"I would prefer a *how was your journey?* first."

"I don't care of you or your journey. Your scroll." Azman placed his hand on the handle of his sword. "Or I'll cut your face off right here."

"Goodness." The man said. Pirouz could not tell if the man was frightened or toying with Azman. "I suppose I will show that scroll then." The man reached into his robe and pulled out a rolled-up scroll, he placed it on the table and unrolled it. There was an image of four snakes attacking a goat. This put Azman at ease; it was what he had been expecting. He gave a grumble.

"You're Jahangir."

"The scroll would suggest so."

"You could have killed Jahangir."

"I don't think Jahangir is that easy to kill, my friend. You're just going to have to trust that I am who I say I am. I understand one being killed for one's scroll is something that happens, but if you think Jahangir is an easy man to kill you are severely mistaken." There was a pause. Pirouz kept his head down, eating the osh but listening intently. The pause seemed to suggest Azman accepted Jahangir's answer.

"Care to extend me the same courtesy? I need to be certain of who you are if this were to work."

"Yes." Azman gulped down half of the osh, placed the bowl down, then pulled his scroll out and unrolled it next to the thin man's. Pirouz could see it had the image of a lion, the sun, and four hawks on the lion's back.

"So nice to meet you, Azman." Azman said nothing. The thin man peeked over to Pirouz and grinned. "I can really use some riches right about now."

"Speaking of which." Azman said.

"Speaking of which *what*?"

"You know which what, pay me."

"Ah yes, of course... about that."

Azman put the now empty bowl down and gave Jahangir a calmly fierce look. "What about it?"

"Oh dear, you are a frightful one, sir."

"This is nothing."

"Oh, I believe you." Jahangir's eyes lit up when he saw the innkeeper come from out of the back of the inn after retreating there long before he arrived. "Sir? What kind of a way of running a business is this? I have been here for quite some time, taunted sir, *taunted*, by the aroma of this most delicious smelling osh. It is a sin sir! A *sin*, to tease me so." The innkeeper smiled and bowed, appreciating Jahangir's playful tone.

"What would you like, sir?"

"Some of this delicious osh, of course."

"Of course!" The innkeeper poured Jahangir a bowl.

After eating, the two men walked outside, Pirouz followed, where he watched Azman viciously beat the smirk off the man's face, pounding his nose, eyes, and mouth into a big bloody pulp to the point where he had no facial features, just swollen, wet inflated purple and red flesh. Pirouz stood back, not knowing what to do. Azman released the man from his grip, letting him fall to the ground, dead. A family of peasants walking past the inn did their best to ignore the scene.

"That man wanted to have you tortured and killed. Everyone here does. I am taking you somewhere where that cannot happen."

It was when they reached the new country that Azman was able to hand off Pirouz to three fellow mercenaries. Their names were Bo, Bai, and Bingwen. They were working for the royal court at the time. It was they who brought Pirouz before his long lost sister and her husband, the emperor. How they went from bandits to monks was another story altogether.

Pirouz, now 18 winters old, was sitting alone in a cave near a violent waterfall, on a mountain full of violent people, with a mission promising nothing but violence and a past that was littered with violent incidents, including the murder of his father. He pondered death. It will come for him. No doubt, he thought. A part of his soul, however, could not shake the horrible feeling that if he never had set foot on this island of hell, he would have lived to see at least another violent day or two.

Chapter 3:
She

Pirouz woke to the smell of tea.

Bai was standing over him, holding a steaming pot of the tea along with a ceramic cup.

"You slept for a day and a half." Bai said.

"Really?" Pirouz yawned, embarrassed. He got up. "I have to go."

"Have some tea and food first. Then go." Bai led Pirouz to the courtyard behind the falls. "I am sorry we quarreled. Had I known who you were, that would not have happened. I have a fond memory of observing you watch a butterfly flutter past you when we took you to see the emperor, when you were but a boy."

"I don't remember a butterfly," Pirouz said.

"I do... it was a simple moment. We were traveling through the city, you saw one and it looked as though you had never seen one before. My brothers and I thought it was very funny to observe because you looked so dopey."

"Thanks!" Pirouz said sarcastically.

"Please, sit." A blanket was laid out in the middle of the marble courtyard, presumably where the three monks would train. There was a breakfast of soy milk and deep-fried dough sticks.

"Wow, this looks good," Pirouz said, sitting before the modest but delicious looking food.

"Thank you. I made it myself, it is the least I can do."

"Where are Bo and Bingwen?"

"They are in the village. Picking up some food for the next few months."

"There's a village here?"

"Yes, as a matter of fact there is." Bai started to pour himself some tea, going into further detail: "Blood and Guts village."

"I never heard of that," Pirouz said, biting into the fried dough.

"It is relatively new, you see. There are many people who are attempting what you are doing, young Pirouz." He sipped his tea and continued: "Not all of them have been noble. In fact, I would say most of them lacked honor and basic decency. The ones that possess a proclivity to one's more selfish and violent nature went from the other side of the mountain to avoid us and the woman who runs the inn, whom you met. Thus, the ones who attempted to take the easy way went from the other side, only to find that none of them could get past *The Crimson Wolf!*"

"*The Crimson Wolf?*" Pirouz said with a mix of anxiety and curiosity. You don't mean the clan, you mean a person?"

"He has been on the mountain for many years. He does not wait to be challenged; he simply slaughters all who get in his path."

"Weapon of choice?"

"He carries a large blade that is bigger than four large men put together. One swing of this and he can take out an entire company of soldiers."

"Great," Pirouz said, ironically.

"Joke all you want, young Pirouz, unfortunately, if you are going to be doing what you are doing, you must face death with the full knowledge that it will, in all likelihood, take you away in but a heartbeat and a breath."

"Well... yeah. Doesn't everyone die?"

"Yes, but not everyone is killed. You *could* turn back."

"No. I can't."

Bai sighed. "Very well. I will direct you on how to reach the village. Despite walking into certain death, it is better to go through the village than to go through the graveyard, which is your only alternative. You want to avoid the *jiangshi* at any cost."

"That's the uh... blood-sucker I was told about?"

"Yes, the blood-suckers are awful, despicable creatures."

"There's more than one?"

"Yes, blood-sucking jiangshi make even more jiangshi."

Pirouz began his trek around to the other half of the mountain feeling well-rested and energized. The ginseng tea gave him a little bit of an extra jump in his step, and he felt he had made peace with the fact that he would most likely die on the island. He made his way down a path that went around the top of the bottom half of the mountain. The path was lined with a wall of trees and an assortment of flowers of almost every color that were completely foreign to Pirouz. On another day, he would have stopped to analyze them and see which ones were poisonous, but today was not that day, he thought. He saw a sign at a fork in the road. "Blood and Guts Village" it said on one sign pointing to one path, "Death" pointed towards another. Pirouz, of course, took the path leading to Blood and Guts Village. Death would come later, he thought.

The sound of people chittering and chattering could be heard just beyond the trees. The path turned a corner, as Pirouz walked it, a dirt road lined with wood huts revealed itself just below a hill. Pirouz stood and looked at it. He could see people walking to and from the little huts, minding their business. It seemed as though everyone walking around the village was armed. Some had common blades under their arms, others had bows and arrows strapped to their backs. Every person looked irritated and angry or calm and conniving.

Pirouz took stock of the situation. *I could just roll through, casually, like one of them. I don't think anyone will bother me if I just mind my business like everyone else.* After sitting at the edge of the hill for several minutes, Pirouz got up and walked down the hill road, leading to the entrance of the village. Two stone dragons stood on each side of the village entrance. Pirouz was alarmed to see a corpse lying dead next to one of the dragons.

"Don't mind him," a crotchety old voice said. "He lost a bet." Pirouz looked to see where the voice was coming from. It was an old man with a beard, holding a jug of what was sure to be wine, sitting on the outer wall of the village. He was either drunk or pretending to be so, a common tactic with some martial warriors.

"That must have been *some* bet," Pirouz said.

"Yes, it was." The old man leapt from the wall to just a few feet across from Pirouz. "But everyone gambles with their lives here. As you are. Why are you here, boy?"

"What do you care, old man?" Pirouz responded.

"It is just not common to see someone so foreign-looking as you to be here. Where are you from, boy?"

"Again, what do you care, old man?"

"Because I am a nosy drunk."

"You're not drunk, you're just playing. I know your type." Pirouz smirked and started walking into town, hoping the old man would follow him so it looked like he wasn't by himself.

"And what type would that be?" The old man asked, following Pirouz as Pirouz had hoped.

"You act all drunk and foolish, just so people can underestimate you, then you break them when you fight. I knew a guy like you. You're a *drunken master*."

"Heh heh heh." The old man cackled. "There are men like me where you are from?" He asked.

"Yeah, there's all types." Pirouz kept walking through the town, everyone it seemed, stared at him and the drunken master as they walked past. *If this old man wasn't with me, I would have been attacked by now,* Pirouz thought as a muscular man holding a large saber eyed him from a food hut with a bowl of greasy noodles in front of him.

"Buy me a drink and I will tell you some secrets!" the old man said.

"Nah, you've had enough, and I don't want to be burdened with your weird secrets." Pirouz said.

"My secrets are the difference between life and death!" The old man said. "There is a tavern just at the end of the road."

"That's great, enjoy your time there," Pirouz said sarcastically.

"I refuse to believe that a boy who has lasted but five minutes on this murderous mountain would be so foolish as to walk out of this village to his certain death."

"What makes you say that, old man?"

"First off, call me by my name. I am Yuen."

"Okay, Yuen, what makes the end of that road *certain death*?"

"My lips are sealed unless you buy me a drink."

Pirouz stopped. "Okay, Yuen, you win."

Pirouz had an assortment of stones and coins in case he needed to buy anyone's loyalty on the island. He shook his silk bag full of them to hear the clinking sound while he sat down at the tavern table with Yuen across from him. The patrons, two men drinking quietly across from one another and the big man with the saber from outside (he decided to step in the second after Pirouz and Yuen arrived) all kept a fraction of an eye on Pirouz and Yuen.

"You've made a fatal error boy," Yuen said gravely.

Pirouz sighed. "Yes, I know."

"The three men are—"

"Plotting to kill me, I know."

"More like they're plotting what they will eat *after* they kill you." He shook his head. "Why in the name of the heavens would you flaunt anything of value here?"

"Because... *I want these idiots to try and <u>kill me!</u>*" He said this with a roar. The two men who were quietly drinking both revealed circular saws attached to long chains. They both swung towards Pirouz, who jumped up from the table right before the saws carved through the wood. Pirouz did a flip and landed on his feet, his sword unsheathed with a flash of light sparking against the blade. He raised and charged toward the two men. One swung the saw back, which Pirouz dodged, causing the blade to saw its way through the man's face, resulting in a bright cherry-red spray of blood to gush forth from his skull. Pirouz sliced the hand off the other man, which fell to the ground, still holding the chain. Pirouz raised the blade and nicked the man's throat with the steel, causing it to mist blood into the air. Pirouz then took another swipe, slashing the man's chest open. The red poured as he dropped to his knees, his ribs split and sticking out of the gaping scarlet slash in his chest.

Pirouz backed away from the now dead man and looked at the big man. "You wanna try me, sir?"

"I would not mind it all, I love killing little brats. I'm the Brat Killer."

"*The Brat Killer*? That's what people call you. That is *so stupid!*" Pirouz tried to sound as much like a brat as he could

Yuen howled with laughter. "This boy is a funny one!" He cackled.

"Get out of here, you old drunk." Brat Killer looked back at the boy. "And no, my name is not Brat Killer, they call me—"

"No, no. It's okay. I don't care. Come here and die." Pirouz said with the utmost arrogance. Brat Killer growled like a tiger and rushed towards Pirouz with his saber up, completely missing him and having his head lopped off in the process. His blood, rich and red, spurted and pumped out of his cleanly cut neck for a few moments before his body clumsily collapsed to the floor like that of a slaughtered lamb. Pirouz looked at Yuen, then the owner of the restaurant. The owner looked new to middle age, like he came to the island seeking riches and instead opened up a food place because that was the only realistic thing he could do now that he was there. "Sorry, sir."

The old man looked flabbergasted at Pirouz. "It's not me you should be sorry to." Pirouz noticed the old man was not looking at him, but over his shoulder. He glanced at Yuen, who also had a nervous look on his face, then behind him, to see a young woman in simple clothes with two scythe like blades in her hands. She looked at the men on the ground, then to Pirouz.

"They killed my parents." She said. "Did *you* just kill them?"

"Yeah, I did. You're very welcome."

"YOU BASTARD!" she screamed, slamming one of the

scythes into a table.

"What, did *you* want to kill them?" Pirouz asked innocently.

"Yes! I would think that's obvious, you *fool!*"

"Fool? That's harsh."

"I was trailing those guys for years! Some might say my whole damned life, I was to get a sweet revenge for murdering my parents, and *you* just had to show up. What are you doing here? Let me guess: You're gonna come here and live your great martial hero adventure and you're gonna come of age on the island because whatever back woods nowhere place you were living had no action."

"That's only a fraction accurate."

"Well, whatever. I hope you die." She stormed out of the restaurant, leaving one of her scythes behind. Pirouz looked at the owner, then to Yuen. He plucked the scythe out of the table and ran out to give it back to her. She was walking down the road at a brisk pace.

"Madame, you left one of your weapons." She stopped, looked at Pirouz in disgust, then snatched it from his hand.

"Give me that," she said as she grabbed it. "I should kill you."

"That's fair." Pirouz nodded his head, his eyes flared, "You think I don't get it, but I do. You deserve your vengeance. *Everyone* does," he said with a nod of the head.

Yuen's voice screeched behind him. "An eye for an eye may leave the world blind, but it sure will be happy! Heheheh." He flipped up into the sky and landed on the village wall.

"He is such a monkey," the woman said. "So annoying."

"You know, that doesn't make sense. Would *you* be happy if you were blind?" She squinted her eyes and shook her head, then stormed back off. Pirouz could see she did not want to have anything to do with him, and so he respected her wishes. He stood in the village square, the passersby were whispering about the fact that Pirouz just killed *the vicious three*. Pirouz could see that while everyone in the village was armed, none of them could match the skills of the men he just killed, thus he was left alone.

"It seems as though you have instantly created a reputation for yourself, boy!" Yuen giggled. "Though I am higher than you, I look up to you. How about you buy me some wine and I tell you stories?"

"What's in it for me?" Pirouz said.

"The friendship of an old man."

Pirouz shrugged. "Fair enough." Yuen jumped off the wall and landed directly in front of Pirouz.

"Do you know the best thing about a village having only one tavern?" he asked.

"No, what?"

"It will always be the *best* tavern around!" Yuen led the way while Pirouz thought about how stupid that last profundity was. So much so, he said, "Old man, that's really stupid." The two walked to the tavern. Pirouz bought him some wine and noticed the tavern owner enjoying a hot pot of tea. He asked if he could bother him for some, which the tavern owner obliged, having just heard of the slaughter Pirouz committed. "So tell me, my drink-loving new friend, what do you know about the Crimson Wolf?"

"Ah, well, you seem like you won't die too quickly under his hand."

"Thank you."

"He is sheer force. It is how he came upon the mask." He sipped some wine and smacked his lips. "Mmmm, that is good. Anyway, the mask belonged to the Crimson Wolf Clan, part of the wolf clan syndicate. We all know the Green Wolf Clan, and how they died. Well, they died mostly by *his* hand."

"Who is *he*?"

"He's a simple thug. He was a foot soldier in the Green Wolf Clan and rose up the ranks before slaughtering his men in exchange for the mask. You see, like any organization, there has always been infighting within the Wolf Syndicate."

"I'm sorry, I am a little ignorant when it comes to the Wolf Syndicate. I know them, but I always found them to be mysterious and confusing. How many wolf clans are there?"

"There's the Crimson Wolf Clan, the Green Wolf Clan, and the Gold Wolf Clan. Each clan operates from a different region. The Crimson Wolves and the Green Wolves are in a constant fight. At least... they *were*, until the Crimson Wolf, as he calls himself, wiped out the Green Wolf Clan to curry favor with the whole Crimson Wolf clan."

"Why'd he do that?"

"Power, silly boy. Do you know of the mask he wears? The mask of the wolf warrior?"

"No, not really. Tell me." Pirouz noticed Yuen's wine cup was empty. "Could I get more wine for my friend, please?"

Yuen's glass was refilled. He took a sip and continued. "The mask of the wolf warrior's origins has always been up to debate. Some say it was created by the Crimson Wolf Clan to conquer the world, and they had it infused with an unspeakable demonic energy by the hands of a wicked heretic warlock. Others say it was created in the heavens by ancient gods who sent it to earth to make all who wear it a righteous warrior. *Other* others say it was created by both good and evil spirits and it gives the one who wears it a choice: To do great acts of good with it, or tremendous, unspeakable acts of evil."

"Hm. I wonder, what if you wanted to just wear it and do your thing? Take a walk, for instance?"

"You really are a fool, aren't you?"

"No, no. I'm joking, of course. What do *you* think, old man? About the mask."

"I think it's a divine gift." Yuen noticed a butterfly flutter past the entrance of the tavern. "Everything is, though."

"That's a nice way to see things, I suppose."

"At any rate, you should go fight him in an hour, that way it will take less time for you to die."

"Why's that?"

"Because that young lady who hates you is going to go fight him. She may fatigue him before he kills her."

"Why is she going to fight him?"

"Revenge, silly boy. The men you killed murdered her parents, but the Crimson Wolf killed her older brother- or so she told me. You see, that girl is from the Green Wolf Clan."

"Really. Damn, I should go." He downed his tea, which had colled, and left the tavern.

"You're going to go fight him? You're not even ready!"

"I can't wait for a woman to be killed in order to fight someone. I don't know- for some reason, it just doesn't feel right."

"Eh, I know what you mean. Have fun, boy! Thanks for the wine!"

Pirouz burst out of the tavern, then remembered he had no idea where to find the Crimson Wolf, so he went back into the tavern, sheepishly. "Where *is* this guy, by the way?"

"He's in the Screaming Forest. Go down the road and take the path that leads out of the village. You can tell you are in the right place because the cicadas will be screaming- hence the name, the Screaming Forest."

"Thank you. Hopefully I see you again. You're pretty fun."

"*If* I see you again, you're stronger than I thought, boy."

Pirouz gave his head a nod and ran out into the village, gripping the handle of his blade. His stomach felt like it was full of air again and his adrenaline was pumping into his brain as he raced past the village square all the way to the end of the road, where the village ended with just a trail leading into the forest. Pirouz stopped. The forest trees formed a wall of green just beyond the road. Pirouz could hear the cicadas humming- indeed, making it sound like the forest was screaming. He stepped onto the trail and kept walking until the sight and sound of Blood and Guts village was far behind him. The trees around the trail were so numerous, they formed a ceiling of green overhead, concealing the sky. The cicadas did not sound like ones Pirouz had heard in his life. It almost sounded like they were warning him.

"I DON'T CARE IF YOU KILL ME, I WILL TAKE YOU WITH ME!" Pirouz could hear the girl scream this. He started to run toward where the screaming was coming from. He could see the figure of the girl holding twin sai blades out with her arms extended. Her face was half red, as Pirouz ran closer, he could see it was from a gash in her face. Standing before her was a beast, a castle of a man who looked to be at least seven hundred pounds of bulky, inhuman muscle. He had two double-sided spears.

"Hi! Can I join the fun?" Pirouz said, stepping out from behind a tree with his sword out.

"You? Buzz off! Don't get in the way of my vengeance again," the girl said.

"Yes, let me kill this little bird, then I will kill you, I would like to savor the taste of this one."

"Ew," Pirouz said. He gave the woman an apologetic, embarrassed smile. "Sorry, madame, I want revenge too, against someone way scarier than this idiot."

"*Okay* then. Go get him and leave us to our death match." The girl said, annoyed.

"Yeah, I don't think I'm gonna do that." He stepped in front of the hulking masked giant. "See, if taking this idiot down is what it takes to be able to slaughter the man who killed my master, I'll take on fifty morons who look just like him, and as fun as *you* are... I'd take on at least five of you." The woman looked shocked to hear this. "Now..." Pirouz looked at the man-beast before him. "COME AT ME WITH EVERYTHING YOU'VE GOT, STUPID!"

"DON'T CALL ME STUPID! YOU KNOW WHO I AM, YOU KNOW WHAT I CAN DO."

"I *don't* know who you are. Who are you? You're just a fat fool in a silly mask." Pirouz twirled his blade around and got into his fighting position.

"I AM THE CRIMSON WOLF, KILLER OF THE GREEN WOLF CLAN, LEADER OF THE CRIMSON WOLF *CLAN*!"

"That's great, thanks for the introduction. Now: LET'S FIGHT." Pirouz flashed his blade forward as the creature human charged at him like a one man stampede. With both double sided spears up, the Crimson Wolf burst forward. Pirouz slammed his sword against the first blade to come his way, clanging it away from him. Pirouz used his lightness kung fu to fly up to a branch of the tree behind him. The woman shot a look at him, fuming.

"My revenge is more important than yours, get lost!"

"Sorry, woman. I already kind of am. Where are we?"

"YOU'RE IN THE SCREAMING FOREST, WHERE YOU WILL DIE!" Crimson Wolf sounded furious. Pirouz could see he was angering the man, so he sat on the branch and moved his legs around, nonchalant.

"Are you sure about that? I feel like... and please don't take offense to this... I feel like if you were going to kill me it would have been done by now, right? I mean, it looks like you and little happy over there have been going at it for a while, am I right?"

With a mighty "GRRRRRRRR" roar that almost sounded like it belonged to a lion, the Crimson Wolf swung both spears in a twirling motion up the tree whose branch Pirouz was sitting on, reducing the tree trunk to a dust cloud of splinters. His spinning blades were about to reach Pirouz on the branch, but Pirouz leaped to the other tree branch before the blade could slice him into ribbons. The top of the tree slammed into the ground and toppled over as Crimson Wolf spun his blades towards the other tree, destroying the tree branch. Pirouz leaped back down to the forest floor, landing next to the girl.

"I'll tire him out, you kill him. I don't care about this idiot." Pirouz said this quickly, then ran towards where Crimson Wolf landed, clashing his sword against the spears, just as the mammoth-like man shook the ground of the forest with the impact of his landing. The two traded blow after blow. Pirouz dodged the tip of the blade, it slid past his eyeball- so close, if he had closed his eyes, it would have sliced his eyelids off. Pirouz did four backflips, making way for the girl to make her attack. Pirouz could see she was skilled as she traded blow after blow with the monster, holding her own against the skills of the wolf. Pirouz jumped back into the fray, leaping behind the wolf, who was so well trained from his years of being a killer he was able to fight both kids at the same time, using both double tipped spears to deflect each of their moves, causing a fireworks display of sparks to flash in the forest air.

Pirouz began his tornado attack, spinning wildly, much like a twister, pounding metal against metal as the Crimson Wolf tried to keep up, with his considerable weight making him much slower than the young prince. The girl used the distraction to her advantage by running up the trunk of the tree behind her, super quick, so she could bounce off of it with her sword in the air, bringing it down on the back of the beast's head, wedging it into his skull. Her hands were gripped on her sword, tightly. Crimson Wolf swung his head around, taking the girl with him as her sword was now stuck in his head, with him still being very much alive. Blood poured down his back. He dropped one of his spears and tried to pull the sword and girl out of his head, but it wasn't easy as his massive arms could barely reach behind his head.

That was when Pirouz sliced his arm off. It was a clean slice, his sword, one of the sharpest blades to be ever used in the House of Poison, was so fine is sliced right through the bone. The arm fell to the ground with a thud, looking like a large piece of raw meat with a stick of bone in the middle. The blood poured down like a bright red geyser. The girl let go of her blade and landed on the ground. She unsheathed a small dagger tied to her leg, jumped up at the crimson monster, and proceeded to stab him repeatedly in the chest and neck. The mutant of a man fell back on top of Pirouz, sending all three of them down a raven, tumbling through branches and trees like a boulder with two small rocks tied to each side.

They all hit the ground, hard, Crimson Wolf's body settled into the dirt, a cloud of dust spread through the air. Pirouz was underneath him. The girl kept stabbing.

"I think he's dead." Pirouz said, worming his way out from under him.

"You..." She jammed the knife into his neck and carved it open like it were a piece of mutton. "...can never be sure." Blood sprayed across her face. She caught her breath.

"I hope you feel better." Pirouz said, dusting himself off.

"I do, actually." She got up and kicked the body. "I feel *real* good to be honest with you. I'm not even mad at you anymore."

"Neat. Well, you're welcome."

"I could have taken him on without your help."

"I'm sure, you would have been an inch away from death I fear, but hey, that's just one guy's assessment of the situation. I could be wrong."

"Whatever." She looked down at the body, then crouched down and ripped his mask off. She smiled. "This is mine now." She held the mask in her hand and smirked, she then went back to a serious face and looked back at Pirouz. "You don't want to fight me for this, do you? 'Cause if you do, I'll kill you. Are we clear on that?"

"Yeah, cool. Take the mask- I don't care. I think it looks dumb, anyway. Just don't tell me you're here for the Savior Sword."

"*You* are here for the Savior Sword?!"

"That is correct, ma'am."

"Hah! Good luck!"

"Thank you! I sense your sincerity and don't detect any sarcasm." Pirouz sheathed his sword. "Have fun getting off the island now that your work here seems to be done." Pirouz noticed the sky was getting pink and purple as the sun was going down again, making room in the sky for a full moon. The crickets began singing for the night, Pirouz noticed that they were surrounded by a field of tombs. It was then that he came to a frightening realization: *We are in the cemetery!* He looked at the woman. "What is your name? You can give me a fake one if you like, I just think I should call you something if we're going to make it out of here alive."

"Why do you say that?"

"Because we are in the cemetery- and no one does."

Chapter 4:
The Old Man and the Cemetery

"My name is Xi," she said, just as a wolf could be heard, howling to the moon from somewhere deeper in the mountain.

"Let's go, If we move fast we can get out of here before it's completely dark." Pirouz started running, briskly. Xi laughed and ran after him.

"Wait, are you for real afraid of the *jiangshi*? You think that's real?!"

"Real or not, I am not keen on finding out."

"It's just nonsense."

"Well, whatever it may be, I don't want to be here. I hate cemeteries and I hate being around dead people."

"That's weird, I love it." She stopped running. Pirouz noticed and stopped running too, looking at her.

"What, you like it so much that you want a jiangshi to drink your blood!?"

Xi laughed. "You actually believe in the jiangshi? It's just a stupid thing made up by old people to scare young ones."

"How could you be so sure of that?"

"Because I've never seen one. When I see one, I'll believe it. You're scared?"

"No! Absolutely not! I am Pirouz, Prince of Persia! I fear nothing!"

"Then why are you running away in such a cowardly manner?"

"How dare you, madame! How dare you! I am simply trying to protect a young, foolish woman!"

"I think I can take care of myself."

"Right, that fight with that big idiot suggests you are

someone who can be totally independent."

"Of course it does! You were simply interfering."

"Look, it was fun meeting you and all, but Madame Xi, I implore you, for your safety: If you got your revenge leave the island now, just go back that way, take a boat and go, what more business do you have in this barrel of snakes?"

"I'm not done!"

"What else do you want to do here? Study the wildlife?"

"I'm not done with my revenge. I want to kill the last of the Crimson Wolf clan."

"Now *that's* funny. You are skilled, I'll give you that, but little young *you* is going to kill the rest of the Crimson Wolf clan?"

"Yes."

"Well, good luck with all that." Pirouz started walking at a steady pace, conserving his energy. Xi scampered next to him, keeping up, amused by his fear.

"You don't find cemeteries fun?"

"No, not at all, madame. I find them horrible."

"Why? They are so peaceful."

"Do you go to cemeteries often?"

"The Green Wolf clan sect I grew up in was stationed near a cemetery."

"That's right, you're a Green Wolf."

"Yes." She put the dead man's mask on and looked at Pirouz. "What do you think?"

Pirouz looked at her and said, sarcastically: "Stunning, it brings out your eyes. It's a bit loose though."

"Thank you, and yes, I agree, the man had a big head. I think it would be even more aesthetically pleasing on *me* if it just covered the eyes, do you agree?"

"Yes, I think—" Before Pirouz could finish what he said, the mask squirmed on Xi's head as though it was alive. Both of them stopped, Xi tried to rip the mask off as it moved like a jellyfish on her head, then shifted its shape to just cover her eyes. They looked at one another, spooked. "Whoa, the mask just changed to how you wanted it to be!"

"Wow that was crazy!" She looked at Pirouz. "I feel like I had fifty cups of ginger tea."

"Really?" Pirouz was even more scared. "You should take it off! What if it's a demon?"

"You are *so* superstitious! This is great!"

"I'm not superstitious, I am just cautious of what is clearly some sort of witchcraft!"

"I'm not a witch! You haven't heard of the Mask of the Crimson Wolf?"

"No!"

"The mask brings out the wolf warrior in all who wear it!"

"That's scary!"

"Jeez, you're very cowardly, aren't you?"

"Look woman, everyone has things they do not like. I do not like spirits and demons and things of that nature. They freak me out!" A wolf howled off in the distance. Pirouz stopped and looked up at the sky. The stars were beginning to twinkle as the sky became black like ink. He looked straight ahead to where another patch of forest began. There was a little hut just on the edge of the cemetery. An old man who looked to be either sixty years old or a hundred was beating a carpet with a broom. He stopped and looked at the two kids approaching him. "Hey old man! Do you live here?" Pirouz asked.

"Yes, yes I do. I tend to the cemetery. You two should not be out right now, the jiangshi will get you." Pirouz ran up to him, Xi followed. "Would you mind if we took refuge in your humble little home?"

"He's scared." Xi said.

"I'm not - just wary, there is a big difference."

"Are you two husband and wife?" The old man asked.

"Gross! No!" Xi said.

The old man laughed. "Oh, you young people with your ways."

"Old man, what's your name?"

"Just call me Old Man, I like that."

"Okay, old man, would you be willing to host us for the

night?"

"He's afraid of the jiangshi." Xi blurted out.

Pirouz looked at her, annoyed. "I fear nothing. Again, I am just a careful individual. It's why I have survived this life for so long!"

The old man cackled. "For so long? You're a baby still!"

"Yeah, this guy is really dramatic," Xi said with a smart-aleck smile.

"I'm not, I'm just a man trying to go about climbing a mountain. No more, no less." Pirouz held up the jar of pickled garlic he got from Auntie. "I have nothing much to offer, but I *do* have this jar of pickled garlic, you can have it - all of it."

The old man held his hand up, refusing the gift. "That is not necessary." He said. "Just keep this old man company. It has been a while since someone made it this far up the mountain." He stepped inside the hut, leading the way for the two kids to join him. The two complied. Pirouz could see that the old man hadn't had a visitor in years. The small space was dusty and the air was stuffy. Pirouz noticed Xi subtly hold her nose behind the old man's back, as the smell was not unbearable but fairly odd and stale. "Do forgive the mess," the old man said. "It has been a few years since my wife died. She kept me tidy. Now I see no point in keeping the place clean. Truth be told, I am just waiting to die since my wife passed."

"Oh wow, that's so dark!" Xi said with amazement.

"I'm sorry to hear that, old man. How long have you been on the island?" Pirouz asked, eyeing the table in the middle of the hut.

"Decades now. Please, sit." The old man extended his frail hand out, inviting them to the table. Xi and Pirouz sat across from one another.

"Old man, how have you survived *here* on the island? I heard this place was jiangshi city."

"Well, the jiangshi can only go inside spaces they have been invited into."

"Really?" Pirouz was fascinated.

"Yes, the jiangshi are ancient creatures of evil, and ancient creatures of evil go by rules little known to man."

"Weird, what other rules are there?"

"Well, they cannot be in the sunlight, otherwise they will burn up into ashes. They must drink blood to sustain themselves, which we all know, and they are just vile! Jiangshi are lowly creatures, for they mimic a human but are slaves to their addiction to human blood!"

"Question: Can a jiangshi just drink animal blood? Does it have to be *human*?" Pirouz asked.

"They can, the jiangshi here sustain themselves by drinking rat blood!"

"Gross!" Xi said.

"The worst thing is when they turn someone into one of them. Usually, a jiangshi will swoop down from the sky, for they jump and fly without the aid of lightness kung fu and pull their victims from the ground like bastard gods!" He shook his head. "It is a sad sight to see, a jiangshi transformation. You forget of all the love you ever had in this world and you just want blood from then on end. They stay in their coffins all day and come out at night. One time I was tending to the cemetery and it got so late that it became night. As I was making my way back home to my wife, a jiangshi gang of about seven chased me until I stumbled and fell into a tunnel I had never seen! The tunnel was white like snow and it had ornaments all along the sides, for whatever reason, the jiangshi dared not to enter! So I stayed there until daytime and when I came out, they were gone for the day."

"Whoa. That's frightening. Why don't you leave?" Pirouz asked.

"Because, young man: I am waiting for my wife. The jiangshi stole her from me."

"Sorry to hear that." Xi said.

"Yeah, old man, that sounds not fun."

"It most certainly isn't." He gave a melancholic sigh. "My wife and I came to this island before it became the notorious mountain of killing and death it now is. We came to have a little life for ourselves. If you ever want to make the universe laugh, however, just tell her your plans."

"So what happened, you came here and the jiangshi swooped her up?"

"Something to that effect. When we first settled here, long before this area was a graveyard, she said that at night, after I would sleep, she would see the jiangshi floating outside."

"It was just one?" Pirouz asked.

"It started as one. A man. He was ghostly white with red eyes that glowed in the night. I thought my wife could have been seeing shapes in the nightly mist that came down on the area, but I saw, one night, while gutting a fish, the jiangshi in all of its horror."

"What was it doing?"

"It just stared and smiled with its horrible, empty, glowing red eyes."

"Did he say anything?"

"No, he just pointed. Then she came out. She was hypnotized, I tell you!"

"How did he swoop her up? He just grabbed her?"

Xi smacked Pirouz on the shoulder and whispered, "That's an insensitive way of wording it."

"Yes, indeed, that is what happened. She came out, and he snatched her up and pulled her off into the mist."

"I'm sorry that happened to you, old man." Xi said.

"What is one to do?"

"Yes, indeed." Xi said.

Pirouz repeated, with a sad nod "Indeed."

The old man stared off into nothing, then smiled. "Have you met the woman who runs the restaurant near the shore?"

"Yes." Pirouz said. "She's a nice lady if she doesn't beat your ass."

The old man nudged a plate of candied fruit toward the two young warriors. "She brings these, every so often. I was a friend of her father."

Pirouz grabbed a piece of candied kiwi and chewed on it. "Thank you, old man." Everyone jumped at the sound of someone, or *something*, collapsing at the door. "What was that?!" Both Pirouz and Xi unsheathed their weapons and got up. The old man put his hand up.

"Do not be alarmed... It's probably a wounded animal." The old man stepped over to the entrance of his hut and pulled the blanket aside. Pirouz and Xi were behind him. A woman was on the ground, bleeding, in a fetal position.

She whispered: "Please, let me in... or they'll kill me."

"Help me bring her in here!" The old man shouted. Pirouz and Xi carried her in by grabbing hold of her arms and feet, then laid her down on the old man's cot. She was whispering incoherently. Pirouz was scared at the sight of her torn, bloody clothing, which was in tatters.

"He's coming... he's coming tonight to finish me." She whispered this, trying to shout but too weak to do so.

"You're safe now, no one's going to hurt you if I'm here." Xi said with authority.

"Yeah, me too," Pirouz added.

"Who is *he*? Who did this to you?"

"The jiangshi... he's vicious... he's killed so many..." She cried. "Now he's gonna kill me..." She sounded hopeless. Tears streamed down her face. Pirouz and Xi both felt it would be unkind to prod her with details of her horrific story. Instead, Pirouz made tea while Xi gave her some of the extra clothes she had brought. The old man drew her a bath in the other room and burned the wood beneath it to make it hot.

"I was going to leave in the morning, but I think I should stay until she's better." Xi said, looking outside the entrance of the hut with Pirouz as the woman bathed in the other room and the old man sat in silence outside.

"Hey, if you're willing to stay, I won't feel bad because I have to go."

"Where do you have to go that's so special?"

"I have to kill the man who killed my master and I have to steal the Savior Sword in his honor."

"Who killed your master?"

"Some bastard in a mask."

"Was he a Crimson Wolf?"

"Nah, I don't think so," Pirouz looked at her and said, in a whisper, "he could be. I don't know, I dunno anything about the *thing*."

"If he was a Crimson Wolf, I'll help out. I wanna kill em all."

"That's fine by me, just let me be the one who pierces his heart."

"If I do, don't get mad." Pirouz gave her a disapproving look, to which she replied: "What? You killed the idiots who killed my parents."

Pirouz shrugged. "Well try not to."

"I'll try."

"Thanks." Pirouz noticed Xi's eyelids getting heavy. "Hey, you're just about passing out, when was the last time you went to sleep?"

"A few nights ago, before coming here."

"Why don't you sleep, I'll be on the lookout, then I'll leave in the morning."

"You think if a jiangshi came in you'd be able to handle it?"

"I'll manage." Pirouz said. "What are you gonna do? After this?"

"I told you, I'm gonna kill the last of the Crimson Wolves."

"You know where to find them?"

"Yeah, I have an idea."

They both said, at the same time: "The Bridge of the Crystal Sparrow."

Pirouz looked at her. "So you know."

"You think I'd be alive on this island this long if I didn't?"

"Yeah, good point." He nudged his head in the direction of the old man, who was now sleeping. "Take a cue from the old man."

Xi yawned. "I'll sleep where she's bathing." She moved away from the entrance, then stopped and turned to face Pirouz. "What was your name?"

"Pirouz."

"Xi."

"Yeah. Sleep well new friend." Pirouz said, she pursed her lips in a friendly way and went back to where the woman was bathing. Pirouz leaned up against the wall of the hut with his hand gripped tightly on the handle of his sword. He was alert at first, but then, as the crickets of the night sang their song, he felt himself get lulled to sleep.

"Where have you been?" The old man's voice gently awoke Pirouz, who at first did not remember where he was or who the voice belonged to. He realized that he had been sleeping on the floor of the hut.

"I was away, my love." Pirouz opened his eye further, noticing a woman's feet standing just before the old man. Her voice sounded soft yet even in a whisper, he could hear her perfectly. "I have seen beautiful things... lovely flowers. There are more flowers on this island than you can imagine. I can show you some."

The old man started cry. "I've been without you for so long." He whimpered.

"Do you remember our life together?" She asked, kneeling down, petting his head.

"Yes, it's all I care to remember. I don't care about anything else. Without you I just want to wait for you or wait for death."

"Sssshhhh." She said, softly. She leaned into him, they were just an inch apart. Pirouz watched silently as she kissed him. His eyes closed, looking lost in the dream of his love. Pirouz looked away.

"Ouch! What are you doing?" Pirouz looked back, the woman seemed to be biting on the old man's tongue, his lips was already bloody from a bite that Pirouz missed. The woman jerked her head back, ripping the tip of the man's tongue out. He fell back, his eyes were big as saucers while the blood dribbled down his chin. Pirouz jumped back out of fear. The woman looked at him, her eyes looked like they were filled with black ink or bile. She hissed, revealing two sharp teeth that almost shot out of her mouth like the fangs of an animal.

"Hello boy, come to me."

"No thank you!" Pirouz stood and whipped his sword out. Xi ran out of her room, looking like she was jolted out of sleep.

"Xi, I think she's a jiangshi!"

"You *think?*" Xi shouted.

"Yeah!" Pirouz shouted back.

The woman shrieked. "You insult me!" She opened her mouth and screamed a scream that sounded like it belonged to a million vile creatures, her teeth looked like a row of jagged sea shells. She jumped toward Pirouz who blocked her with his sheath. He fell from the sheer force, stumbling on his back then shooting back up to his feet, swinging his sword several times at the she-beast, who dodged each one without even looking like she was moving. Xi charged at her with blades up, but each swing was dodged with ease by the jiangshi lady. She leaped to the ceiling and crawled like a spider to the other side of the hut. She stopped, her head cracked and made a snapping sound as it turned to fully face behind her. "You look like you will taste sweeter than the other one." Her voice slithered out the words like a beast speaking from 7 hells.

"My love, stop this! Come with me, we'll leave the island!"

"Shut up you old fool!"

"Hey, old man, don't let her talk to you like that!" Pirouz shouted. "Plus, sir, do think that's *still* your wife?"

"Shut up, boy." The old man grumbled this while still transfixed on the contorted woman in the corner of the hut.

"He's not seeing what we see," Xi said "He's seeing what he remembers." Pirouz looked at the bloodied old man, he was now looking calm and docile. The woman leapt off the corner of the ceiling and stepped towards him. Xi and Pirouz ran toward the two. Xi stepped between the woman and the old man. "Old man, this is unhealthy."

"Mind your business, brat!"

"No! You! You hurt him and you're only going to hurt him more if we let you. Go haunt someone else."

"He's mine!"

"Come and get him, then!" She put her twin sais up and ran their blades across each other, causing a spark to shoot out and hit the jiangshi woman.

"Show off!" the jiangshi shouted, then leaped towards Xi with her hands up, Pirouz did a somersault on the floor, blocking her path with his sword. She stopped right before the blade could touch her face. She smiled, revealing every sharp tooth in her head. "I think the others should join in on the fun!" She bent backwards, once again mimicking the shape and movements of a spider, and crawled out of the hut, skimming past Xi and Pirouz with super speed. Before they knew it, she was out the door.

"Wow, that was awful, right?" Pirouz sounded beyond spooked - so spooked he could only state the obvious.

"Yeah, I would say that was not good," Xi said, sounding a bit less shaken.

"And now she's gonna get more, that's *really* not good."

"What say we do? You wanna split?"

"Split to where? It's dark out, we don't know how many of those things are out there." Xi looked at the old man, who was stammering to himself words they couldn't quite hear. "Old man? That tunnel you mentioned is still around, I assume?"

The old man looked at them. "Yes." He began to mumble, "It was her, it was her, my love is not dead!"

"Where are they?" Xi asked.

"Where we used to have picnics. Oh the picnics we would have!"

"Tell us where that is, we'll take you there so you can have a picnic with her," Pirouz said, Xi smacked his shoulder.

"Don't enable his fantasies."

"We need to get there somehow, who cares? Look at him, he's half gone." He looked at the ground. "What if we dug to it?"

"Are you stupid?" Xi asked this sincerely.

"Honestly? Only when I'm scared, one of my shifus told me this."

"We have to just run out to wherever the old man says the tunnels are. We can just run out of here. Old man, where do the tunnels lead to?"

"The Garden of Eternal Winter... out the other end is Suicide Peak... where we used to go and look at sunsets..."

"C'mon, let's go." Xi said, heading outside. "Old man, you should come too."

"I am fine here." He collapsed to the floor. Xi and Pirouz rushed to help him sit up. Xi said, as they did so: "We can't just leave him here to die."

"Okay, I volunteer to carry him on my back."

"I *can*." Xi said.

"Don't worry about it. My shifu, Master Míngzé, would have wanted me to do that. C'mon, old man." Pirouz held his arms out to try and pick him up.

"No..." The old man smacked Pirouz's arms away. "I have to wait for her."

"OLD MAN! SHE WANTS TO KILL YOU! LOOK AT YOUR MOUTH!" Pirouz shouted.

Xi placed her hand, gently, on Pirouz's shoulder. "He wants to stay here... let him."

Pirouz and Xi left the hut, leaving the old man behind. They rushed through the night, careful not to trip over the various gravestones.

"Is that it?" Pirouz pointed to the entrance to a large marble square with a gate in front of it.

"No, that's some tomb, it's further. It's a little light ball, you see it?" Xi pointed to further out in the distance. Pirouz squinted while he ran. He could see what she was referring to. Just to where another part of the mountain began, there was a hole in the rocks that had light coming from it. A loud crash reverberated through the cemetery, shaking the gravestones. The doors to the tomb burst open. Jiangshi, a swarm of them, all of them with their razor teeth out and blank, black eyes shining in the moonlight, leapt from the tomb entrance, then towards Pirouz and Xi. The two young warriors brought their weapons up and proceeded to slice every jiangshi that came their way. Xi's twin Sai tore across every passing jiangshi, resulting in geysers of blood spraying out of the passing wounds. Pirouz performed a hurricane attack offensive, slicing off limbs and heads until the last jiangshi was split in half from the waist. Pirouz and Xi were bloody and had their weapons still up as the blood mist cleared, and they saw that all of the jiangshi were scattered about, either de-limbed or disemboweled or decapitated.

Pirouz and Xi looked around, making sure every last one of them were dead.

"Let's go." Xi said. Just as she started run towards the light in the rock in the far-off distance, one of the arms on the ground grabbed a hold of her ankle. Pirouz was shocked to see a bodyless limb move on its own. He raised his sword when the top torso of one of the jiangshi catapulted itself at him and snatched his sword clean from his hand.

"Hey you bastard give me that back!" Pirouz backed up to the tomb walls. He saw that the jiangshi's body parts were rejoining themselves. A jiangshi whose head had just zipped back to his body jumped up towards Pirouz. Not having any other weapon to defend himself save for his poison needle and his dagger, Pirouz took his bag and swung it at the jiangshi's head. The jar of pickled garlic cracked, releasing the garlic and vinegar in the bag. The jiangshi held his head, shaken from the trauma. Pirouz hit him again, the head of the jiangshi began to fizz with a green, acidic mist. The skin of the jiangshi turned red as green bubbles ate away at him, causing him to finally lose all life, collapse, and die. Pirouz looked at the bag, then raced out to where Xi was busy re-hacking the jiangshi that were circling around her.

Pirouz swung the bag like a spiked ball and chain, hitting every jiangshi in his way with it, causing their heads to burn into a green mist that exposed their red, gory insides. He pounded the bag down on the various heads and limbs on the ground, burning them up into green acid puddles. Xi sliced the last one up, cutting the top half of its head off, severing it right at the eyeballs. The head spun away from it, Pirouz raised the bag over his head and swung it down, smashing it into the red gushing wound of the jiangshi. It crackled with larger green bubbles than the rest and dropped to its knees, then fell forward, lifeless. Pirouz and Xi looked around to see that they were all dead. The two ran towards the tunnel. Pirouz retrieved his sword from a dead jiangshi on his way. The closer the tunnel got, the stranger it appeared to them. It was lit with candles and seemed to be made of snow and ice.

They reached it after five minutes of running as fast as they could and ran inside and stopped. "This place is... amazing." Xi said, inspired by the beauty of the tunnel, the walls of which were white, glistening rock covered in various blue and white diamond-looking stones that lit the entire tunnel up. Pirouz and Xi both touched the walls. Pirouz tapped on one of the diamonds in the stone. "You think you can take these off?"

"No... you can't." Pirouz and Xi looked outside the tunnel, the edge of the graveyard, and saw a man with long hair and a pale face that had two red eyes glowing out of them. "Many people have tried, they just give up, go out the other end of that tunnel, and get killed. I've seen it one million times."

"Who are you?" Xi asked. "Aside from being of those blood sucking freaks?"

"I am the leader of those blood sucking freaks." He took a few steps forward. "There are many more of them, and they already don't like you, and I'm none too sure how long that little bag of garlic will last against an entire army of my followers."

"We'll just have to find out for ourselves." Pirouz raised the bag.

The man chuckled softly to himself and put his hand up. "You need not worry. I have much bigger fish to fry on this island. Just consider this a fair warning: Stay away, I cannot promise you will be as lucky as you were tonight." A green mist formed around the man. He said as he disappeared into it: "Also, the old man is dead and with us now."

Chapter 5:
The Garden of Eternal Winter

After saying that, the mist evaporated, and he was gone.

"I need a second to collect my thoughts," Pirouz said.

"I feel the same way, but I say let's go in further... it reeks of death here." Xi started walking deeper into the tunnel, Pirouz followed. It began to feel like the coldest of winters was waiting for them on the other side of the tunnel, which was long and shimmering with shiny rocks that were stuck on the walls.

"It looks like someone slammed a perfectly circular hammer into the center of the mountain and it just went clean through- like a hammer with a sharp outer edge," Pirouz said, sounding amazed.

"Yeah, the walls are so perfect and smooth," Xi said.

The tunnel curved a bit. As they walked and their breath fogged the air, a voice sounded off, revealing itself to belong to a man sitting on a rock, right where the tunnel ended. Outside, it was snowing. He was looking at the falling snow with a serene look on his face. "Welcome to the Garden of Eternal Winter."

Pirouz could tell who this man was just by looking at him: The shimmering, white clothing, the gaunt face, the long white hair, and the fingernails that were sharp, crystal-looking, and curved, this was none other than Ice Snake, the famed martial hero who lived in the Garden of Eternal Winter, where there was always snow. Pirouz pounded his fist into his palm and bowed. "I am a member of the House of Poison, sir! I wish no disrespect, but we wish to pass through the garden of eternal winter, if it is no trouble to you, sir!"

"You may." He stood up and looked at Pirouz and Xi. "At

your own peril."

This shocked Pirouz. "Ice Snake! I was told by my shifu that you were a fair and just man! We mean you no harm by being here!" Pirouz shouted this but was still respectful in his tone. "We have just fought and killed many jiangshi and would like to just peacefully pass through!"

A contemptuous sneer washed over Ice Snake's face. "Disgusting, the jiangshi certainly are the pests of the island. Worse than the rats." He got off the rock and looked at Pirouz, then smiled. "You're the little prince." He chuckled. "Pirouz, I believe your name was?"

Xi looked at Pirouz. "What does he mean by *little prince?*"

"People are who they are, I suppose." Pirouz knew not what else to say but that. He was what he was. He was the little prince. He turned his attention back to Ice Snake. "Yes, I am he. Pirouz, son of Yazdegerd, member of the House of Poison."

"I heard about Míngzé, it's a shame. I've seen the bastard that did it here, many times."

"Do you know him?"

"I wouldn't say I *know* him. We see each other, we fight, that type of thing." He made a disgusted look and shook his head. "Whoever that masked man is he is quite good. I have yet to meet someone more skilled."

"I am here to avenge Míngzé, I know his killer is here. If I get killed avenging him, so be it."

"Well, you *could* get killed not avenging him at all, have you thought of that?"

"Yes, when one goes on a quest for revenge, this fact is meditated upon for days."

"Please, I'm not one of your shifus at the House of Poison. I am Ice Snake. I care not for your reverence, just be honest with me. So you have thought of this man or woman killing you?"

"I don't think that's going to happen."

"I think it will."

"I don't."

"Well I do."

"Not if my plan works."

"What's your plan?"

"I will pierce his heart with the Savior Sword. If I have that sword I will be sure to kill him."

"Ha, that's funny, and I will kill every clan on the planet, I just need to pull the moon from the sky and do that. Give me a moment, which, by the way, do you even *have* the Savior Sword?"

"Well, no, not now."

"I see. So you are going to go retrieve the hardest-to-obtain object in the world, and then you will kill the man who killed your shifu. Then what? You two will get married?"

Xi cringed. "Gross! No!"

"We just kind of are standing next to each other, I feel nothing for her."

"Sure."

"Ice Snake, why do you not wish me to kill the man who killed your friend? Míngzé spoke highly of you."

"It's not that I don't wish you to kill him, it's that I just do not think that is possible. I have fought the thing; he is insane in how he moves, both insane and precise, a lethal combination." Ice Snake walked to the edge of the tunnel. He motioned for Pirouz and Xi to join him. The three of them looked out at the trees and falling snow and an ice lake and the countless icicles that hung from every branch. The beauty was awe-inspiring. "It's not even that masked weirdo I am worried about, it is more this garden. It seems I am the only one who has been able to survive it."

"What do you mean?" Pirouz asked this, then turned when he noticed the sound of footsteps clopping toward them from where he and Xi come from. Ten men holding arrows and blades, and hunting equipment and mean looks on their faces, stepped up to them and stopped.

"Are you that Ice Snake fella?" The man in the middle asked, who was bigger than the others.

"Yes, yes I am."

"I expect you'll let us pass. We want to see what all the fuss has been about."

"You will get no resistance from me, friend." Ice Snake gracefully extended his hand.

The big man who seemed to lead the others chuckled. "In another life, Ice Snake, I would have loved to test and compare our martial skills against one another, but today I am just a hunter, here to see the *thing* that has been so thirsty for blood!"

"I appreciate that, new friend. What is your name, good sir?"

"I am Lixin, the hunter! These men are my fellow hunters, I have led them on *many* successful expeditions!"

"I wish you and your men luck. Please, go about your journey." Ice Snake and Lixin both pounded their fists together and gave the other man a bow, then Lixin led his men out of the cave and into the garden of eternal winter. Pirouz noticed a smile crack across Ice Snake's face.

"It's a pity, he seemed like a rather pleasant fellow."

"What was he referring to? What is he hunting?" As Pirouz asked this, he watched Lixin the hunter and his men disappear into a snow-frosted cluster of trees, disappearing.

"The thing that is going to make him and his men scream, then die." Ice Snake put his hand up with his index finger sticking out. "Wait for it." The first screams sounded like they came from three of the men, followed by the sound of flesh being torn and bones being crushed, many at a time. Then the screams sounded like it was coming from a few more, followed by more tearing sounds and bone crunching, then a howl from Lixin the hunter and the sound of his skull getting cracked. Pirouz knew that sound because he had heard it before. "And that was the story of Lixin the Hunter and his men." Ice Snake's eyes looked like he had seen this many times and was now bored by it. He floated down to the garden from the cave, lightly touching down on the snow, then started walking to the cluster of white trees, where the screaming came from.

Xi looked at Pirouz. "Are you spooked out?"

Pirouz shrugged. "Not really. I'm too mentally exhausted from this island to be." Pirouz used his lightness kung fu to float down to the garden and follow Ice Snake, Xi did the same.

Ice Snake began telling the tale of what he knew, providing Pirouz and Xi with some context. "I come to the garden once a year to meditate and collect my thoughts. I stay for a month, as I have many thoughts to collect." He stopped and crouched down. "It was on my latest excursion that I found this:" He dusted off some snow, revealing the frozen, anguished disembodied face of a dead man. His skin was white and blue and it looked as though it was a face that had been torn off the rest of his body, which was heaven knows where.

"What happened to *him*?" Xi asked, morbidly curious.

"The *Snow Thing*."

"The *Snow Thing*?" Pirouz repeated this, now getting even more spooked as he was lying when Xi asked him if he was earlier.

"From what I have gathered..." Ice Snake pointed to a crater in the snow leading to the cluster of trees. "It's a big thing." Pirouz realized what he was actually looking at: It was a footprint, a big one.

"That's very interesting, I have to go now." Pirouz remained facing forward but used his lightness kung fu to float backward, back to the cave.

"Hold on." Xi said and went back to where Pirouz was. "So you *are* spooked! You're such a scaredy-cat!"

"I *am*, okay? I fear no man! But I just hate creatures and demons and ghosts and jiangshi and all of those things the way people hate rats and other vermin."

"So what are you gonna do?"

"What are *you* gonna do? You didn't find those screams and the footprint not to be inviting?"

"Oh, the screams weren't enough for you?"

"That's when I thought it was a really skilled human. I was literally picturing just a really big *person*, not a *Snow Thing*! *Whatever* that is!"

"Okay, well, it was nice meeting you I guess." She shrugged.

"Wait, is this goodbye?"

"Well, yeah. I wanna go get my revenge on the rest of the Crimson Wolves and you want to do your thing, which is cower, I guess, no disrespect, so there you have it." She pursed her lips and nodded her head, then floated back down to Ice Snake, who began to walk into the mini forest, where the screams came from. Pirouz thought to himself for a moment, then floated back down to join Xi and Ice Snake.

"Wait for me! Sorry, I thought I forgot something up there, but we're good!" Pirouz noticed Xi trying to conceal a sly smile when she heard him say this.

"Kids, let us discover what gruesome things your new friend the Snow Thing has done now." Ice Snake led the way into the forest, where, just a few steps in, the carnage began. The blood from all of the men smeared across the snow, steaming a red cloud of mist. Pirouz noticed all of the intestines strewn about the red lake of blood and limbs thrown about among the bodies. "Poor Lixin." Ice Snake said, pointing to Lixin's body, whose head was squished and purple with his eyeballs popped out, dangling from their red connective flesh strings.

"Snow Thing's bloodlust has been satiated today. He kills, then goes off to his hiding place. That's why we are safe. He is fed."

"*Fed*?" Pirouz said, pointing to the gore pile. "What did he eat? It's all here in this pile of guts."

"He probably ate a liver or a kidney, he was just snacking. Despite his size, he is actually a very light eater! He simply likes to rip things up and run away." He sniffed the air. "He went down the well." Ice Snake pointed to a large well. The footprints led to it, the blood spots getting less and less as they reached the brick well. "If it weren't for this blasted well, I could find him easier, but there is no way I am going in this thing". A growl echoed from down below. "Don't let him alarm you. He gets cranky and sleepy when he is well fed. He'll be down there for a while. He is very shy and evasive when he's not ripping people up." He pounded the ice-slicked rocks of the well. "Drat. With the way things are developing, he will be hiding for days." Pirouz was pleased to hear this- that was, until Ice Snake whispered, "Now we just have to worry about the mother and father."

"Mother and father?" Pirouz asked.

"That's right."

"Are they bigger?"

"Yes, they are, by a significant margin." Ice Snake smiled. "I bet, like me, you cannot wait to see such a beast!"

"No, actually, quite the opposite, I am eager not to," Pirouz said.

"Well, I do not share that sentiment, young man. I am, in fact, a *yaoguai* hunter."

"Really?!" Pirouz was shocked. "When did this happen? Master Míngzé said you were just one of the great masters. Why would you go off and become a yaoguai hunter?"

Ice Snake gave Pirouz a deathly serious look. "Did you know how many names there are for yaoguai? *Monster, beast, creature, unnameable,* to name a few."

"Yeah, so what?"

"That's all fascinating! Follow me!" Ice Snake used lightness kung fu to jump up to the top of the trees that formed an ice dome. "Look here. Do you see this?" Pirouz and Xi hopped upwards to the branches above, joining him. He was pointing at several branches, which appeared to be crushed. "The creatures climb the trees. Yet they are so heavy! Fascinating! Absolutely fascinating!"

"So what are your plans for this *snow thing*?"

"I want to domesticate him."

"Ha! You want to domesticate a *monster!*" Pirouz had heard of Ice Snake's *foolish optimism* as Míngzé put it. It was interesting seeing it happen before his very eyes.

"Young boy, can you imagine how wondrous that would be? Ice Snake and his army of snow things?"

"What makes you think you can domesticate such a beast? The trial and error involved could be lethal." Xi hopped over to the next branch over. "If you need help, I would not mind lending a hand. I have an interest in yaoguai."

"Absolutely, young lady, I could use all the help I can get."

"As much as I would love to help you find a bloodthirsty creature, I actually have some vengeance to exact. Is there a shortcut to get out of here?"

"Yes, young man, there is. Follow me." Ice Snake floated back down to the snowy ground below, Xi and Pirouz followed him. "Just cut through the trees, go between the two mountains, and just keep walking. You will reach a valley that leads to the trail leading up."

"Thank you, Ice Snake." Pirouz pounded his fist into his palm and bowed, then looked at Xi. "Have fun monster hunting."

"I will. Good luck on the rest of your journey." The two pounded their fists into their palms and bowed. Pirouz started to walk away, hearing chatter as he left.

"They truly are fascinating creatures, these snow things..." Pirouz could hear Ice Snake rattle off facts (like "I saw one drinking water from the frozen lake by cracking it open!" *etc...*) as he walked away, deep into the forest. He would have liked to stay with Xi more, but he had to make his way. As he walked deeper into the frosted forest, the sounds of Xi and Ice Snake disappeared, leaving him only with the sound of the cold breeze blowing through the ice-caked trees. Music hummed through the forest. Pirouz stopped. His feet crunched over the frozen leaves and twigs on the ground. He noticed a figure crouched on a tree branch, playing a flute, which was the source of the music. He jumped from the branch, twirling in the air, then landed just a short distance from Pirouz.

"This is the end of the line, boy." The old man had a big, scruffy white beard. "I am afraid it is now time for you to die."

Pirouz unsheathed his sword. "*I* am afraid now is not the most convenient time for me to die."

"I wouldn't be so sure of that, boy." The old man pulled a large spear with a curved blade from behind his back. He spun it around and slammed the tip of the spear into the snow, causing the snow to ripple. Pirouz jumped up to avoid the aftershock of the ground moving, then landed on his feet with his sword raised.

"Who are you, old man?" Pirouz shouted, demanding to know who was trying to kill him.

"I am the *Yaoguai Master*!" The old man shouted maniacally. "I have been stalking that idiot Ice Snake since he got here!" A growl came from behind the trees. Pirouz could see eyes- eyes that glowed red- staring at him from the trees behind the old man.

"I don't want to kill an old man, old man."

"That is a shame, boy, because this old man wants to kill *you*!" The old man made a forward motion with his hand, causing the growling eyes to come out, revealing the fearsome blue and white furred face and freakish body they belonged to. The creatures looked like a cross between a rabid dog, a gorilla, a bear, and a pig. Their bodies were covered in fur while the flesh around their monstrous faces was wrinkled slabs of blue, fleshy, hairless skin. They charged at Pirouz, who shot into the tree above him, then to the next, then to the next as the frothing animals followed him, chipping away at the wood as they climbed. Pirouz knew he had to warn Ice Snake and Xi. He sprinted forward to the highest tips of the trees, then bounced from treetop to treetop. He noticed the beasts had climbed back down and were now making their way towards Pirouz's new acquaintance.

As Pirouz slammed down into the snow, that very moment, the two beasts stopped, sat, and looked at Xi and Ice Snake, like hungry but obedient dogs.

"Heh, heh, heh." The Yaoguai Master crunched through the snow as he stomped over to face Ice Snake, Xi, and Pirouz. "Well, Ice Snake, we finally meet."

"You must be the Yaoguai Master."

"Yes, I am."

"Well, as you know, I am Ice Snake."

"Yes, I know. You have been snooping around this garden, being annoying."

"I would like to ask you about the purchase of one of your lovely beasts- along with domestication tips!"

"Feh! Just go! You are so annoying! I am but the beast master, I need no friends!" The old man croaked this at the top of his lungs.

"Old man, I wasn't asking for a friend, in fact I was hoping-" Ice Snake's face changed suddenly, he powered into the old man right as a flaming arrow hit the tree behind him. Ice Snake fired up to his feet. Xi and Pirouz got into their fighting stances. A grizzled mound of fat and muscle and thick animal furs stood holding a flaming arrow along with a torch hung over his shoulder.

"Yaoguai Master, stand down! For it is I! Shuchang the Hunter! I have come to claim the lives of the snow things!"

"You will have to go through me first, Shuchang." Ice Snake said.

"I see that. Do you accept my challenge?"

"I do."

The old man hissed at the two snow things, which scampered away, back into the mini forest. "I will find them, old man. Make no mistake about that. In the meantime: Whom do I have the pleasure of challenging?"

"I am Ice Snake, surely you have heard of me."

"Yes, it is not difficult to hear of a peacock that hits people."

"What is that supposed to mean?" Ice Snake sounded offended but was smiling.

"It means you are a flamboyant sort."

"And what sort might you be?"

The man slammed a large mallet on the ground, shaking the earth a bit. "I am simply a man."

Pirouz and Xi did not know what to do, so Pirouz asked: "Should we just chill and watch?"

"I guess," Xi said.

"Will we be using weapons or fists? I assume this is a death match?"

"I don't know any other way to fight, to be quite honest

with you, big man."

"Wonderful, it is settled then! I will crush and murder you, then I will take the skins of the snow things!" He removed his animal pelts and tossed them on the snow.

"Are we doing this then?" Ice Snake asked, stepping up towards Shuchang.

"Yes, we absolutely are." His muscles bulged as he put his fists up and squeezed them, causing his veins to pop out. "I am not a fan of peacocks."

"Well, that's a shame." Ice Snake got into his fighting stance. "But in answer to your question I think we're both in the mood to beat each other with our bare hands. Sound good?"

"It will be my pleasure." He motioned his fist towards him. "Come here and get your death beating." The two men ran at each other and traded blows, the snow on their clothes powdered in the air as their fists, arms, and forearms pounded against each other in a flurry storm of punches. Ice Snake slyly stepped aside, causing Shuchang's fist to hit nothing but air just over his shoulder. Ice Snake moved again, causing Shuchang to nearly fall over, but keep his balance. Ice Snake pulled off an air kick, smacking Shuchang clean in the face with his foot, causing a smack sound that reverberated across the garden. Shuchang swung his fist like a ball and chain, sending his knuckles straight toward Ice Snake's head, who simply dodged it and landed several blows at Shuchang's chest before backing off. "Hold still and die!" Shuchang screamed.

"I want to give you the same chance I gave all the other men I killed." Ice Snake leapt up and landed three more kicks at Shuchang's chest, slamming his back into a tree, causing the icicles from the branches to come shimmering down. Ice Snake turned to face Pirouz and Xi.

"I think we'll be done quite soon," Ice Snake said this with a grin.

"YES! WE WILL!" Shuchang tackled Ice Snake and jammed an icicle into his neck. He got off of him.

"ICE SNAKE!" Pirouz shouted.

"Ice Snake is no more!" Shuchang said. Ice Snake stood up, his hand floated above the base of the icicle, the base of which was sticking out of his neck, looking like pink glass from the blood. "Allow me to pull that out for you." Shuchang grabbed the icicle and yanked it out of Ice Snake's throat, causing blood to stream and spray out, painting the white snow in a deep and rich red. Ice Snake fell to the ground, face first.

"COWARD! HE WAS UNARMED!" Pirouz shouted.

"Oh, is that so, boy?" Shuchang cracked his knuckles. "Come here and we can chat more about your theories of combat."

"Leave these stupid kids alone, you brute!" The old man shouted this, then leapt up into the tree. "And I will never part with my snow things! I will have them eat your eyeballs and kidneys before I let you harm them!" The old man backflipped into the forest, disappearing into the woods.

"Don't listen to the old man. Don't leave me alone, because I want to beat you to death for being a coward."

"You talk far too big for such a little boy, *boy!*"

"Come here and die, bastard!" Pirouz darted towards Shuchang like a hawk, sword up. Shuchang took out a stone attached to a chain, swung it around, and knocked Pirouz upside the head with it. Pirouz spun around and muttered to himself, before everything went black: "That was a lucky shot, you bastard." He could feel something warm streaming down his face. It was blood, and he fell.

In the blackness, Pirouz began to hear a fire going. He opened his eyes, feeling like he had been out for a week. Pirouz was lying down, bound. Before him, Shuchang the hunter was cooking a whole chicken over a fire, humming to himself. Pirouz turned his head to see his surroundings. Shuchang had made a snow home around them. Pirouz turned behind him to see Xi, with her back to him, bound and bundled in pelts.

"I can sense you are awake. There is no point in trying to wake *her*, she hasn't moved in a while. She may be dead." He laughed, then faced Pirouz, holding the whole chicken in his hands. He took a big bite of the chicken's flesh and ripped it out, chewing on the white meat and skin. "My plan is to attract the old man and the snow things with her screams." He took a swig of wine from a large jug. "I used to be a torturer. For various people." He inched himself towards Pirouz. "Being a torturer is interesting, to say the least. I used to like just beating people to death when I had an enforcement position, but I kind of just drifted into torture. Before that, though, I kept it simple. I used to like strangling my victims. You know what they don't tell you about strangling?"

"No, what?" Pirouz was curious, even in his unenviable position.

"The tongue."

"What about it?"

"It sticks out of the mouth, like it hangs like a slug coming out of your head. Like this." He stuck his tongue out, mimicking his victims. "It's quite funny to see." He stood up. "One thing that's quite fun is cutting things off, then burning the wound so they stay alive longer. I find sewing them back up is a bit cumbersome and unnecessary if you're burning them with a hot piece of metal."

"Do your plans for us involve the hot metal you speak of?" Pirouz asked.

"Oh yes." He reached into the fire and pulled out a red-hot knife, glowing orange at the tip. "What I was thinking was cutting off your sensitive bits. Those elicit a certain type of scream. Then I'm gonna make you whimper, a steady, annoying whine, then hopefully the snow things will want to kill you and put you out of your misery. That or the old man, or both."

"You seem to think the snow thing master and us are good friends or something."

"Well, I saw you with him."

"I've been in the same space as a lot of people, that doesn't mean I'm super friends with everyone."

"Hm. I'm still carrying on with my plan."

Pirouz could feel his straps that were used to bound his wrists together behind his back. It was a leather piece of rope.

If he kept stalling, he may be able to loosen them, he thought.

"I tortured a guy once." Pirouz said, matter-of-factly.

"Oh really? Do tell me about it, was it fun?"

"It had its fun moments." He tried to position himself more comfortably but gave up. "You see, I'm from the House of Poison. Yes, *the* House of Poison,"

"Oh yeah, I've heard of them. Wild group they are."

"Yeah, they're pretty wild. Myself and a friend were charged with killing someone who tried to poison one of our masters. We tortured him for a day before he died."

"What did you do?"

"Well, we wanted to know whose orders he was working off of. So we did glass torture on him."

"I am a fan of glass torture." Shuchang said. "How would you go about it?"

"How does one go about glass torture? How anyone does, I suppose. You take some ground-up glass and grind it up, put it on the floor, then toss the lucky person to it and lets the pain do the rest." Pirouz chuckled. "I hope I'm not giving you any ideas!" The two laughed.

"No, no. I have a plan. What I was thinking was having her wake up to your screams."

"Forgive me for asking, but how would you elicit those screams?"

"That's a good question, just broken bones and the one or two odd cutting off of prized body parts."

"Oh, good heavens, that sounds like a good start!" Pirouz said, sounding like an excited kid. "Listen, Shuchang, truth be told, I am actually on your side: I hated Ice Snake. I was on a mission to come here and kill him, and here's the really crazy thing: I came here to aid whoever wanted to find and capture the snow things! Isn't that just a wild coincidence?"

"But I want to kill the snow things."

"Well, I support that. Question: why do you want to do that?"

"To make myself the finest hunting outfit in the world."

"Oh, okay." Pirouz smiled. "How about you untie me and

untie her, and we go find those things, eh, pops?"

"I actually had another plan: I torture you to death…" He held up the red-hot knife. "Then I have my way with her and hope her screams for mercy draw out those stupid animals!"

"I have an issue with that plan." Pirouz said, his wrist straps were not getting any looser.

"What are your issues with the plan, boy? The torture you to death part?"

"No, it just lacks humanity, it's not nice basically. It's not a *nice* plan."

"Well, one shouldn't judge something before they experience it." He tossed the red-hot knife into his other hand. "It's beyond *not nice,* however. The way I hurt people is more mathematical. Let us begin." He stepped towards Pirouz with a tight smile that looked like he was going to savor every severing of every nerve. "Do kindly turn facing me." Pirouz spat in his face. "Turn facing me damn you." He punched Pirouz in the head. Pirouz remained conscious but could feel his eyes getting heavy. "Damn you! Don't pass out, you must feel everything!" Shuchang brought the knife down below Pirouz's waist, ready to burn off whatever was there, when he jerked forward and grunted a confused, throaty sound. He turned around. The end of an arrow sticking out of his back nearly took Pirouz's eye out when he swung around. Xi stood by the entrance of the snow home, holding up her bow which had just been shot. She already had another arrow strung up and ready to go by the time Shuchang rammed toward her. The arrow went directly into his eyeball and into his brain. He fell, dead.

Xi screamed, ran towards Shuchang's unmoving body, and stabbed him over and over with a hunting blade she ripped from a strap on his pelt. Pirouz watched the stabbing go on and on until his chest was nothing more than a gaping hole of gore. "I think he's dead." Pirouz said.

Xi caught her breath. "He tied us both up and made this ice home. Then he got very drunk and I was able to break loose and leave a decoy. The fact that he wanted to *have his way* with me made me kill him with more hatred than I would kill anyone else."

"I see." Pirouz said. "Can you untie me?"

"Sure." Xi flipped Pirouz over and sliced the straps off of his wrists. Pirouz savored the feeling of having them free. He snatched the knife from Xi's hands and sliced off the straps on his feet. Pirouz leapt up and stood, then felt dizzy. "Careful, you were out for a while."

"Yeah everything feels spinny."

"C'mon." Xi led the way outside. The snow was falling, heavy.

"Did the old man come back?" Pirouz asked. Just then, he noticed something shiny and red, dusted by the snow. It was the old man, the creature master, dead, in a frozen circle of blood.

"He killed the old man. He hunted him down like a dog and killed him." Xi sounded sad that this happened. She stopped when a sudden shrieking howl pierced the air of the night. "Wait here." Xi went back into the snow home and changed into her snow gear and got back out. Another shriek hissed through the garden. "We have to hurry. Try to keep up."

Pirouz and Xi ran through the snow. "The bridge is just beyond a ravine separating the garden from the rest of the mountain." Pirouz said this while huffing and puffing as he ran.

"Yeah I know. We can make it if we just---" She stopped at the sight of red balls of light, off in the darkness. Pirouz froze along with her. It was quite clear that the red, glowing balls of light, were the snow things, waiting for their prey to move. "Don't move." Xi whispered.

Pirouz whispered back, "Don't worry, I won't. I'm too scared to." The eyes stood perfectly still. Xi took another step. Her foot crunched in the snow.

"If we move slowly maybe they won't... kill us," Xi said this in a hushed tone. They moved, slowly. Still, the eyes remained fixed on them. The sound of their feet crunching through the snow- even with the sound of the storm- was deafening to hear, knowing it could lead to them being ripped limb from limb. It was after twenty steps- and still not so much as a blink from the red glowing eyes that the two reached a wall of darkness.

"I think we made it," Pirouz said, relieved. The sound of a grunting gave way when the two saw the eyes bobbing up and down as the snow beasts came into view. The snow beasts jumped up, claws out, teeth shining in the moonlight, ready to tear the two kids apart.

Chapter 6:
Cruel Captain Ru

Pirouz made a grand leap into the darkness, as did Xi, without knowing where they were going. Having no aid from their lightness kung fu, they fell down the ravine, pounding through snow-covered branches and rocks, then smacked down on the lake below, which was half ice and half water-right where the Garden of Eternal Winter ended. Pirouz was on his back; he could see the glowing red eyes looking down on them from high above. They blinked, then lost interest and went away.

"You okay?" Pirouz asked, wincing from the pain.

"I'm doing great." Xi was also on her back, staring up at the moon.

"So... you still feel like fighting the Crimson Wolf clan?"

"Not now, but I still want to do it." She moved her head to look at him. "And who said anything about fighting? I want to *kill* them."

"I just figured this whole experience would make one fatigued."

"Yeah, welcome to life." She sat up. "The bridge is just past the trees."

"I would take a rest. Not from your vengeance," he said, sitting up and groaning, "just from, you know, strenuous physical activities. Otherwise, you'll march right to your death."

She sighed. "True." She noticed a rabbit on the other side of the lake, where the weather stopped being winter, and the trees and bushes were lush and green. "I'm starving. Rabbit sounds good right about now." She looked at Pirouz. "Do you like rabbit?"

"I could eat one of those snow things right now, that's how hungry I am, but rabbit is fine too." The two got up, brushed themselves off, then walked along the edge of the lake, out of the official parameters of the Garden of Eternal Winter and into the area of the mountain where it was, like the rest of the mountain, spring.

"Do you want to set up camp? Or did you want to keep going?"

"Are you asking because *you* wanted to set up camp?"

"I was going to. Once we're further from the garden."

"Sounds good," Pirouz said, getting up to continue to walk up the mountain. "I hope to find a place to rest and meditate - this has all been a lot."

"What do you expect from a place called *Murder Mountain?*"

"True." Pirouz caught sight of a white crane flying toward the trees just past the lake. For a moment, it reminded him of the crystal sparrow scarf he wanted to return, and he thought of the woman he wanted to return it to. He became lost in this thought, then regained his focus and kept walking. "Funny, Murder Mountain can be so visually striking."

"You've never seen a crane before?"

"I have... it's just... I suppose I never thought about how strange they are." He looked at her with confused eyes. "Isn't *everything* strange when you think about it?" He looked at his fingers. "Like fingers, aren't fingers weird?"

"I think that Shuchang guy drugged you and you may be feeling the aftereffects of that."

"Yeah, I do feel groggy."

The two found an area within the forest across the lake that was flat and had rabbits and squirrels running left and right. Pirouz made a fire, fighting through his grogginess, while Xi managed to hunt down two rabbits with her bow and arrow. She was tempted to hunt down several more, but she was far too hungry. She held them up to show off to Pirouz as she walked back. Pirouz was sitting by the fire, he looked at her and smiled.

"You skin yours I'll skin mine and we can roast them." She tossed one of the dead rabbits in Pirouz's hands.

"I was thinking the same thing." Pirouz looked at the rabbit. "Thank you little guy, I hope you had a fulfilling life." The two skinned and gutted the rabbits, chatting as they did so.

"I was debating on the ducks by the lake or the rabbit, but I think this was the good call."

"I agree, I prefer rabbit."

"Really? I like duck myself. Poultry I'm a big fan of."

"What about beef and pork?"

"No, not a fan."

"Hm, interesting." Pirouz stuck his knife into the tree behind him and found some sticks that were thick enough to be used as spits for the rabbit carcasses. As the fire crackled and cooked the rabbit flesh, Pirouz and Xi sat in silence. Night was beginning again, and it was difficult for them to believe another full day has passed.

Xi finally asked: "Do *you* think you're going to die here?"

"I'm not insane, I know there's a strong possibility." He smiled wearily. "It's not like the island isn't completely hostile, right?" Pirouz suddenly got tense, as did Xi, they both put their hands up, sensing a presence from within the forest.

"Someone is here." Xi whispered.

"I know, we're being spied on." The two of them got up to their feet and in their respective fighting stances, sword and sai out.

"Come out, coward!" Xi whispered this in a hiss. The two circled around the fire, scanning the trees around them to spot the culprit. A leaf fell on Pirouz's face. He looked up and noticed a man in a red mask up in the tree above him. The man used lightness kung fu to the next tree over. "GET HIM!" Xi shouted. Both of them ran up the tree and practically flew across each branch, gaining on the man who looked to be jumping for his life. Pirouz tackled the person midair, causing him to crash back down to the ground of the forest, both of them bashing through tree branches as Pirouz held onto the spy tightly. They slammed to the ground with the spy below Pirouz. Xi landed softly and snatched the spy from under Pirouz, wrestled him to his feet, then stuck the spike of her sai into his neck, puncturing the skin just slightly. It released a thin stream of blood. Xi ripped off the mask. It was just a boy, younger than both Pirouz and Xi, he had a fat, innocent face and looked to be practically in tears. "You're a spy for the Crimson Wolf Clan, are you not?"

"Yes," the boy said.

"You were going to tell them I was here, yes?"

"Yes," he cried. "Please don't kill me."

"It's not up to you or me, it's up to whether the heavens will allow me to cut your throat out. Provided a giant rock doesn't fall from the sky... I think killing you is what fate wants." She was about to jam the spike deeper into his throat before Pirouz held up his hand.

"Wait," he said.

"Wait for what?"

"He's just a boy." Pirouz examined the boy further. "He's a *stupid* boy."

"So what? The world could do with less of them."

"I agree, it's just... you could just tie him up and let him think about being a part of a vicious clan, though I would think this kid was born into it."

"If we tie him, he'll probably die too."

"Then just let him go."

"If we let him go, he's going to go tell the Crimson Wolves."

"True," Pirouz said. He looked at the kid. "Did you come here because you were sent here by the Wolves?"

"Yes," the kid said. "They knew she killed our guy back near the village and they want to keep tabs on her, then kill her. You too, because you killed our guy, too."

"That makes sense." Pirouz sheathed his sword and sat on a rock looking thoughtful. "What say we do?"

"I say what we do: we cut his throat, then you let me go and kill them and whatever you want to do you can do."

"I don't know about that."

"What's wrong with that?"

"He just looks like a little boy is all."

"Little boy or no, we let him go, the entire Crimson Wolf Clan will be here."

Pirouz paced back a forth. He did not want to kill a kid. Xi's passionate hatred of the clan made her want to act with no mercy. "I still think tying him up and leaving him somewhere is better, or forcing him to run to the other direction."

"How long can you force someone to run? You're gonna follow him?"

"No, not at all. We'll just trust his word."

"This boy is in the Crimson Wolf Clan- his word means *nothing*." Xi sounded like she was full of venom. She pointed her sai at the boy. "You look old enough to have a conscience, do you not see how *vile* your clan is?"

"I'm sorry, ma'am," the boy said respectfully. He then sobbed. "I *will not* notify the clan. I will just go down to the village and find a boat ride off the island."

"I will never trust the word of a Crimson Wolf." Xi said this, and through a sudden onslaught of tears, croaked out the words: "You people killed my family." Pirouz could see she was emotional, so he simply stood back and let her compose herself, looking embarrassed that she showed emotion. She raised her sai. "You are a part of the clan that killed my kin, and so, boy, you will die." She ran towards the boy and was just about to stab the point of her weapon in his face when his sudden crying and sobbing made her stop. He began to kowtow to her.

"Please, madame! My clan has done you wrong! I disavow them! They simply took me in when I had nothing! But I curse them now! Please, madame! Show me mercy!" Pirouz could see the tears streaming down his face along with a stream of snot that dripped down his mouth as the boy pleaded for his life. Xi raised her weapon higher. Her hand shook as she held it up. She then put it down.

"Get up," Xi said. "Walk." She shoved the boy by his shoulders. He began walking; she started following him.

"Where are you going?"

"He's going to take me to them."

"Are you crazy?"

"No, I'm blood thirsty."

"You're going to take on the entire Crimson Wolf Clan on your own?"

"Weren't you looking to go up to the tip-top of this hellish mountain?"

"Yeah, I am."

"You gotta kill your way up then. Including the Crimson Wolf Clan. I'm not even saying you should fight with *me*, I would prefer I do this on my own."

"No offense to your skills, but you'll at least get a few limbs cut off, not to mention dead."

"What was your plan? You were going to be friends with them, break bread, and hope they let you past them?"

"I was going to sneak past!"

"Wow, what a coward."

"Oh, that's not nice."

"Walk kid."

"Okay, just don't stick me with that thing."

"It's the thing that's going to slaughter your whole clan. Keep walking." Xi kept her weapon at his throat. Pirouz followed them.

"How far away are they?" Pirouz said.

"Not too far."

"Are you related to someone of high rank?" Xi asked.

"No, I am just a commoner. The son of commoners."

"Really? Are they in the clan?"

"No."

"Where are mommy and daddy? In a nice little village waiting for their little boy to return?"

"No, they are dead."

There was a pause, then Xi asked: "How did they die?"

"The Crimson Wolf killed them."

There was another pause, then Xi asked, "So why did you join them?"

"I had nowhere else to go and they said they would kill me if I didn't."

Xi stopped. "Hold on." Everyone stopped. "Let's eat first. I don't want those rabbits to go to waste." They walked back to the fire, where the rabbits were getting blackened by the flames. Xi took hers off the fire by holding the stick. Pirouz did the same.

"Can I sit?" the boy asked.

"Yes, you may." Xi and Pirouz sat on their rocks as the boy made a space for himself just in front of Xi and sat down. Xi blew on the smoking rabbit meat. "What's your name, boy?" Xi asked.

"I am Da."

"Tell me, Da, do you enjoy helping the people who killed your family?"

"I don't know."

"You don't know. Are you just a dope?" She ripped a piece of meat from the rabbit and popped it in her mouth. The smoke wafted out of her mouth as she spoke. "I imagine I would have conflicting feelings about it, but that's just me."

"Can I ask you something?" Pirouz felt the need to speak up. "What *is* the big difference between the Crimson Wolves and the Green Wolves? You guys are both clans that like to..." He smiled slyly. "... do your thing."

"We don't do anything now, most of the Green Wolves are dead, you ass."

"Sorry, sorry. That was insensitive of me, I apologize." Pirouz pursed his lips and nodded. He noticed Xi still giving him a dirty look. "I'm sorry!" He said again, defensively. He added, for levity's sake, "If you were looking at me wearing that Crimson Wolf mask I wouldn't be able to handle it." He looked at the boy and smiled. "You know she killed the Crimson Wolf? Well, technically, we both did."

"Yeah, that's why I'm here."

"Are they really mad about it?" Xi asked this with a grin.

"It was very shocking!" The boy said.

"You're really dopey," Xi said, stating a fact.

"That's what everyone says. I think I'm smart, though."

"Are you, though? You joined the clan that killed your family!"

"I get where he's coming from, though. I remember when

my dad was killed, I just went with whatever adult pushed me around and smuggled me about."

"*I* didn't. I was a Green Wolf." Xi's anger simmered under her words. Pirouz thought to himself: *What was the difference between a Green Wolf and a Crimson Wolf.* As though she were reading his mind, Xi shot at him: "I know all about your little gang."

Pirouz smirked. "My *little gang?*"

"Yeah. It's your clothes, and the way you move."

"What about them?"

"You're in the House of Poison."

"I accept that the way I move you may think that, for I am skilled and great, but what about my clothes?"

"My mother once told me members of the House of Poison tend to dress flashy." She bit into more rabbit and said with her mouth full: "We never had any problems with them but my mother told me to always watch out for them."

"I have no clue as to what you are saying. *The House of Poison?* I don't even know what that is."

The boy piped in, "Are you really?"

"No."

"If he was, he wouldn't admit to it. Unless he's a dope."

"I'm a dope."

Xi gave an agreeing smile. "You are, I agree with you."

"Kid." Pirouz let out a manly grunt. "I don't know what *The House of Poison* is. That sounds like an odd group. Why would you want to be a house of such a thing? Poison is bad!"

"I actually think you're not dumb." Xi said.

"Thank you! That is so kind of you to say!"

"You're great at *playing* dumb."

"What do you mean?" Pirouz sounded innocent when he asked this.

"Oh *please.* It's a tactic I find tiresome."

"There's no tactic here, madame, just a guy going up a mountain."

"A guy *attempting* to go up a mountain."

"Well, time will tell how this all goes, I suppose." Pirouz

did not want to argue with Xi. He felt bad that her family was killed. "I hope you wish me luck, though."

"Sure, why not." Xi looked at the boy. "Who is the captain in this pack?"

"Captain Ru." The boy said.

Pirouz stopped smiling. "What did you say?" He asked.

"Captain Ru." The boy said.

Pirouz's eyes squinted. Xi noticed his mood had changed. "Does this captain Ru have a scar across his face?"

"Yeah! He does! How did you know?"

"And the scar is a slash across his face, from here to here?" He pointed to the top of his head and slashed it diagonally down his face to his jugular.

"Yeah, exactly like that. He has a crystal eye." The boy said.

Pirouz nodded his head, thinking for a moment. He bit into the rabbit carcass and chewed vigorously. He began scarfing the rabbit down, like a hungry animal. In between chewing, he said "Let's go after we eat." Pirouz thought about the incident that made him hate Ru, forever. It was a vile thing and Pirouz hated thinking about it, yet, as he ate the rabbit, he couldn't help but remember.

It was just a few years ago, before Pirouz experienced his little growth spurt, when he was just a little runt that seemed to be tolerated by the rest of The House Of Poison. Pirouz and Ru were walking to a restaurant where they had heard there was a new chef from out of town that was wowing the locals.

"Míngzé has us doing stupid stuff." Ru said, sounding bitter as always.

"If the master wants us to try some food I am not against it. I am hungry hungry!" Pirouz slapped his stomach. "I need food in my belly! It's dinner time!"

"Stop it, you're being more annoying than usual." Ru said this contemptuously; he hated Pirouz and was sure Pirouz would hate him when he was old enough. Ru was right between the ages of young Pirouz and Master Míngzé and the rest of the masters. He did not have the patience the others had with Pirouz. "Walk in a straight line." He said to Pirouz, who was walking up the road in a zigzag.

"I can't, it's hard for me." This enraged Ru. He would have struck Pirouz if it weren't for Míngzé and the masters.

"Míngzé said for you to listen to me- so listen."

"Alright, Ru." Pirouz walked in a straight line until they reached the little hut which had a small line of hungry towns-people waiting to be served.

"Damnit, a line."

"Ru, why are you always angry? I noticed you never smile or laugh and you only like sad things and vicious things."

"It's not your place to ask such a thing, you vile creature."

Pirouz would have kept going, but he was not in the mood to absorb Ru's abuse, so he shut up. Ru caught sight of the men in the hut. One was taking orders, the other was in the back, cooking ribbons of beef and steamed vegetables. Ru smiled and said to Pirouz, like it were a joke, "The chef is sim-ple." Pirouz looked at the chef. He did seem, from what Pir-ouz could see, to be, indeed, *simple*. From his childlike man-nerisms to his serious focus on his tasks, Pirouz could see it. Yet, unlike Ru, he did not find it funny.

"So what, Ru." Pirouz was embarrassed Ru would bring that up as something to ridicule.

"When I was a boy, nothing was funnier than a simple person."

"Well, you're not a boy anymore, so stop it," Pirouz said.

"Excuse me?"

"Master Míngzé told me that the simple are very close to the spirit world and we should be nice to them."

"Master Míngzé seems to have a great loyal pet in you, boy."

"Whatever, Ru. You would give your eyeballs to be Master Míngzé."

"Shut up Pirouz. You're talking too much and too freely again."

Pirouz said nothing. Ru continued:

"The same way you are with the other masters, you must be with me. Understand that. When I am no longer a student, and I am promoted to running things, you will be sorry you were so... relaxed with me." Pirouz bit his tongue. He was quite used to Ru pontificating on the way things would be once he advanced.

"Give us your special. Two." Ru said, rudely, to the man taking the money. The man nodded his head and put two fingers up. The chef smiled at Ru, then gave an even bigger smile to Pirouz. Pirouz smiled back and waved.

The bowls were served. Pirouz and Ru stood and started to eat. Pirouz was enjoying the meat, thinking about how good it tasted, while Ru picked at it, nibbling. "It's not that good." He said. Two women, one in blue, the other pink, were enjoying their food. Ru gave both his standard, lecherous look. "I know finer places to dine than this charity, madame. I could show you."

"Disgusting, no." The woman in pink said.

"Yes, I can tell you are a bore, leave us be." Said the woman in blue. They went about talking, laughing.

"The other place is *much* better." Ru said.

"I think it's pretty good." Pirouz said.

"What do you know, you have mongrel tastes."

Pirouz said nothing back and kept eating with enthusiasm. Ru kept eating but with a snobby face on the whole time.

"This is the last order we are taking, thank you all," The brother who was taking the orders shouted this. The line of people groaned. "Sorry, sorry. Tomorrow is another day! Thank you!" The man pulled down the curtain of the hut, the line in front of the place dispersed.

"He acts like he's a street performer," Ru muttered under his breath. Pirouz and Ru continued to eat, Pirouz noticed the brothers walk out of the back of the hut. The two women stopped them.

"This is amazing." Said the woman in blue.

"Truly. We are bringing our fathers here tomorrow!"

"How wonderful," the simple chef said. "I will do my best

tomorrow."

"Oh, how sweet." The woman in pink was almost dying from the kindness of the simple chef. "You are a darling."

The other brother did a half bow to the woman and said, "we look forward to serving you tomorrow, ladies."

Ru seemed to simmer with rage as this exchange went on. He shouted "You are not some noble martial hero, stop acting like you walk on the clouds because you can set meat on fire, simpletons."

"Excuse me?" The brother who took orders looked at Ru first in disbelief, then adjusted to what was happening. "Are you talking to us?"

"There seem to be only two simpletons who set meat on fire, no?"

The brother who seemed to run the operation stepped up to Ru. "I know not who you are, but watch how you speak of us." Ru swiftly pulled the man's arm and snapped it behind his back, breaking it. The simple brother ran at Ru like a charging elephant, angry on behalf of his brother. Ru grabbed a hold of the man, lifted him in the air and tossed him, then kicked him so that he flew toward the feet of the women in pink and blue. The simple man began to cry from the pain. Pirouz found the image of the simple man crying to be upsetting and the sight of Ru standing over the chaos he had just caused to be angering. So, Pirouz pulled out the blade the Míngzé had entrusted him with when he became a student at the House of Poison and jumped up at Ru's face and gave him a deep diagonal slash.

"You little bastard! You cut my face!"

"You're being mean for no reason!" Pirouz shouted.

"Come here! I'm going to kill you!" Ru tried to capture Pirouz in his arms, looking like a wounded cheetah still trying to capture its prey, but Pirouz was far too quick. He was practically halfway back to the House of Poison temple before Ru lost his breath and had to walk the rest of the way.

Having beaten Ru to the temple, Pirouz was able to tell his side of the story to Master Míngzé first. Ru arrived and downplayed the fact that he instigated the entire exchange that led to the brothers being attacked by him. The high council of The House of Poison had a trial and came to the judgment that Ru be expelled from the House of Poison with no further punishment. Míngzé located where the brothers lived and gave them a handsome compensation for their troubles. Pirouz went with Míngzé because he wanted to see if the brothers were okay. The brother with the arm injury was healing, and the other one seemed to not remember or care about the events. Instead, he prepared tea for Míngzé, Pirouz, and his brother, and the three pontificated on how some people were just cruel in nature, as Pirouz listened.

Pirouz, Xi, and the boy were marching over to the bridge where the Crimson Wolf Clan was known to be.

"Are you ready to die?" Xi asked Pirouz.

"Did you see much blood as a young one?" Pirouz asked in response.

"Yeah, I did," Xi said.

"Well, you should know that when you see lots of blood when you're young being ready to die is just the way you live."

They walked through the forest; the mist was blanketing the forest floor. "Now *is* a good time to attack. They're all probably drunk or sleeping," Xi said.

"How do you know they're not just waiting for us?" Pirouz urgently whispered.

"I *don't* know. Hence possibly walking into death."

"Are you guys going to the bridge?"

"No, are you kidding?" Pirouz said. "If we set foot on The Bridge of the Crystal Sparrow, or even near it, we'll be ambushed by the Crimson Wolves." The bridge- its name a coincidence with the scarf Pirouz carried, was yet another zone of death on the island.

"I know a way in," Xi said. "It was my original plan."

Pirouz looked at Xi. "Care to share?"

"No, not in front of the boy. Just follow me." Xi looked back at Pirouz. "Have you ever done shadow kills before?"

"Yes, as a matter of fact, I have."

"That's how we must go about this. The longer we can spill their blood in the darkness, the better."

"I happen to agree." Pirouz reached into his sack and pulled out his shadow mask. The boy looked at it in awe. It had eyes like mirrors that made Pirouz look like a sly and deadly bug and the fabric around it covered all of his face. It was greenish blue material that blended in with whatever was around it.

Xi noticed the mask and had to say: "A star shadow mask?"

"Yeah, no big deal."

"Where'd you get it?"

"It's a long story." Pirouz said as they continued to walk.

Xi stopped in front of a towering tree. The camp was close enough that you could hear the chatter and the roaring fires of the Crimson Wolf clan. "This is the end of the line, boy." She took some rope out of her sack and tied the boy to it. "I hate to waste my rope on you." After tying him up, she took the mask she had inherited from killing *the* Crimson Wolf. Both youngsters now had their masks on.

"See ya around, kid." Pirouz said. "You're lucky I was here, otherwise she would have killed you so be considerate and don't scream."

"I'm not trusting him not to." She tied his mouth with a rag.

"Sorry boy." Pirouz said, sincerely.

Pirouz and Xi left the boy tied to the tree and began to step softly and quietly through the forest, then stopped three trees down. Xi pointed up. Taking the signal, Pirouz jumped up into the trees, Xi went up another.

They both stopped and used their lightness kung fu to get to the very top, sticking to the tips of the trees so that they were invisible in the night. They could both see the watch towers off in the distance. Pirouz squinted to get a better look. He reached into his sack and pulled out a looking glass that Míngzé welded into a foldable tube. Now he could see the watch towers like they were right in front of them. There were two men in each tower. As he had heard and sometimes seen with the Crimson Wolves, they were all wearing red.

Pirouz and Xi looked at one another, gave a nod, then leapt to the next tree, then the other, then the other. They reached the edge of the forest. They both looked down.

There was some chatter going on below. They could see two men standing guard, one with a cup in his hand.

"Yeah, I told him if you want gold for that, fine, but I am not giving my life's fortune for a boat ride that I can do on my own."

"What'd he say?"

"He went on to the next idiot."

The men sounded quite drunk. Pirouz noticed the jugs of alcohol behind them. They were stacked up in a pyramid. Beyond that, they could see the rest of the camp:

The Bridge of the Crystal Sparrow was heavily guarded, they could see where it led to their headquarters. It was a little mini village of wood huts with men and women in red walking around or sitting outside their little homes. There were men who appeared to be the clan muscle on every side of the open area where the huts were lined, including the two drunk men chatting. While Xi scanned the entire camp, her eyes sharp like those of a hawk under the red mask, Pirouz did the same but made sure to be on the extra lookout for Ru, repulsed by the fact that he earned the title of captain within this particular clan. *I should be looking under the dirt because the guy was a worm*, Pirouz thought to himself.

Without warning, Xi jumped down the tree with her twin sai out and sliced at the two men the second her feet touched the ground. She cut their necks in such a way that the blood flooded their throats making it impossible for them to scream. Instead, they hit the ground and were yanked quickly by Xi and thrown behind one of the thick red trees. *How reckless,* Pirouz thought. Xi ran back up the tree. "I'm going to take out the watch towers. Then you do your thing, I'll join you."

Xi nodded. Pirouz leapt from tree to tree, silently in the night, then stopped when one of the watch towers was but a short distance away. Now was the best time to use sleeping poison, Pirouz thought, for his real quarrel, if there was one was with Ru. He threw the needle, it pierced through the air and hit the Crimson Wolf guard in the watch tower. The guard stopped moving for a moment and put his hand up as the needle spread the poison through his neck. The guard collapsed, sounding like a bag of rocks hitting the wood floor of the watch tower. Pirouz used his lightness kung fu through the next series of trees until he was at about the same distance of the other watch tower, one of four planted around the camp. The guard seemed alert and was scanning the camp dutifully. Pirouz got nervous for Xi. He looked below. She was nowhere in sight and the camp seemed to have the same relaxed but alert vibe.

"The boy hasn't returned, has he?" Pirouz could hear two men below the trees, talking.

"No, he is useless. If he does return with no news Captain Ru will skin him alive." This made Pirouz's blood boil. He pulled out another sleeping needle and threw it at the guard in the tower, hitting him in the face, right below the eye. The side of his face drooped down and the guard fell forward. Pirouz was alarmed when he realized the guard would fall over and crash into the guards below. *Don't fall, damnit,* Pirouz thought to himself, his training was such that he barely cracked a sweat when fighting, but right now, he could feel the beads of it gathering under his mask as he prayed to the heavens that the guard not fall over. The guard tilted forward, he fell, Pirouz darted from the tree, gliding over the two guards below, and caught the watch tower guard, flinging him as quietly as he could into the tower.

Pirouz landed in the cabin of the tower crouched down with his hand up to keep his balance. He heard drums going off in the distance. Pirouz thought to himself that it was typical of the Crimson Wolves to have some sort of festival at this time of night. *The House of Poison* is an order, the Crimson Wolves were just a large gang of bandits, Pirouz thought to himself. He peeked his head over the edge of the cabin. He noticed the shine of a man in ostentatious armor walking along the perimeter of the camp. The armor was golden, and his helmet too was gilded. Two men walked on each side as they spoke. Pirouz could not hear what they were saying. As they walked into the center of the camp, Pirouz could feel his gut telling him that that was Ru. *Well Ru, you have made yourself Captain, how wonderful for you.* Pirouz wished he could say that to Ru, right then, with full sarcasm. It was then that the thought presented itself, and it infected his brain and soul. As he watched the man in the gilded armor stop in the middle of the camp, pointing at the men playing drums while the others drank, he hoped for the man to remove his mask. *If it is Ru, I will challenge him right here and now, if I am killed by he or his men, so be it.* As the man in gilded armor turned around to point out to his men another area of the camp, presumably for security reasons, he removed his mask. *Turn around, you bastard.* It was in that moment that Pirouz thought that was when the man turned around, revealing the unmistakable face of Ru. The scar that Pirouz had given him all those years ago was visible from up on high where Pirouz was.

Pirouz's eyes, which appeared red from the mask, squinted, then looked at the next watch tower over. A guard was smoking a pipe. Pirouz, without giving a second's thought, jumped over to the tower. The guard tried to scream, but Pirouz smashed his mouth with the handle of his blade, then smacked the side of his skull with it while it was still sheathed. The guards fell, Pirouz let him fall, his face smacking against the wood of the cabin floor with a nasty crack. Pirouz looked out at the camp. Two guards were dragging in a bruised and broken man whose face was almost featureless from his facial wounds, which swelled up his face in a purple black, and red mound of flesh. His eyes were underneath the puffy wounds, so beaten they could not open. Pirouz was now close enough that he could hear Captain Ru, who was waiting for the men to bring the nearly dead man before him.

"Captain Ru! We caught this man trying to trespass. We suspect him to be with the Green Wolf clan!"

"Nonsense, we wiped them all out."

"But look!" The Crimson Wolf soldier holding up the left side of the injured man ripped a part of the man's sleeve off, revealing a Green Wolf Clan tattoo, which was right in the center of his bicep.

"Ahhh." Captain Ru said. "The Green Wolves are like the worst of insects. Once you think you have killed them all, one hundred others come buzzing about to take their place. It is quite annoying." Captain Ru stepped closer to the bloodied man. "Are you people not tired of the feeling of being hunted down, extinct? You could be living wonderful little meaningless lives on some land, far far away, but no, instead you insist on your silly revenge which will bring you nothing but torture." He shook his head. "It's pitiful, really."

"What shall we do with this one?" The guard to the left of the prisoner asked, holding up a dagger. "I can cut his throat now."

"No no." Captain Ru said. "Allow me." He raised his sword and slid the blade out of its sheathe and swung it down towards the man who let out a squeal of fear. Just as the blade was piercing the face of the crying man, Xi glided through the camp with her twin sai out and stopped the blade with a mighty, fiery clang of the steel in her hands. Pirouz, seeing this go down, took it as his cue to jump into the fray. He did a twirl in the air as his blade became unsheathed. Three guards in front of him held their spears up, Pirouz assaulted them with a lightning storm of sword thrusts that were so powerful and precise they snapped off the tips of their spears. The end of his sword neatly nicked each man's wrist in a whirlwind-like motion, resulting in bright cherry red blood pouring out of their wounds as they panicked and tried to hold the blood in. The wounded guards cleared the way from Pirouz who was eager to get to Ru.

"Ru! It's the little idiot you used to hate! Come here! Now that we are an equal match! Unless you're a coward..." Xi meanwhile had just stabbed the two guards holding the prisoner in their faces, causing more blood to spray and pour down to the camp grounds. The two men ran like cowards as

Xi zipped backwards in her fighting stance.

Pirouz noticed three guards gaze upon Xi, then run. This confused Pirouz for a moment, then the two guards who charged towards him with their spears out brought him back to the action. He bashed his sword against the points of their spears, knocking both men off balance. One of them got up, then saw Xi charge towards her, then kowtow almost suddenly. Xi looked at Pirouz, who glanced back at her, then to Ru, who unsheathed his sword and swung. "I can imagine those idiots at the House of Poison sent you here for some sort of silly mission, perhaps they got tired of you, little idiot."

Pirouz went at Ru with the force and energy of a roaring demon. Their swords slammed into each other so hard that blue sparks flashed between the steel. Xi's twin sai spun in her hands then sliced at more oncoming guards, jumping onto their spears then puncturing them directly into the face causing streams of blood to squirt into the air. Pirouz and Ru were trading blow after blow with a fierce speed that out maneuvered everyone around them. Ru found an opening and managed to get his blade to poke into Pirouz's shoulder. Pirouz growled and used Ru's opening to stab him in his side, right between the cracks of his golden armor. Pirouz did a back flip and kicked Ru in the chest with both feet, pushing him back.

Pirouz touched his wound, blood was pouring out. Just as he noticed the red river running down his armor, he noticed Xi take a spear hit to her arm. Blood hissed out in a spray. Pirouz thought to himself: *A member of the House of Poison is always prepared to die...*

"Mongrels die mongrel deaths!" Ru shouted. Pirouz was backing away as Ru felt the blood under his arm. "You pierced nothing important, stupid boy. You can't even maim properly!"

"Shut... your... MOUTH!!!" Pirouz rammed himself back towards Ru, aiming for his neck, hoping he could crunch up his armor with his sword and break his neck. He swung, Ru dodged it. Xi was clutching her wound, backing up from the oncoming guards like a wounded crane. She noticed half of the Crimson Wolves charging at her, the others looking on at her reverently. Pirouz nearly fell over as he missed striking Ru. Ru raised his sword and brought it down on Pirouz's neck. Right before the blade could meet the back of Pirouz's head, Xi blocked it, holding up her twin sai, her blood poured on Pirouz's face as he turned to look up. Pirouz moved from under Xi and they crept slowly away from the army of men and women holding up spears. They pressed their backs to one another tightly.

"If this is the end." Xi said.

Pirouz finished her thought: "It was nice meeting you."

Chapter 7:
Beware the Skull Crusher

Pirouz and Xi saw the murderous intent in everyone surrounding them. Yet even in the heat of the moment, they were confused by a small fraction of them; They seemed to be kowtowing to Xi. Ru's armor clanked as he rushed at the two. Something from the night sky zapped itself into the dirt between the two young warriors and the killer in gold and caused the dirt to explode. Pirouz and Xi immediately knew what it was: an exploding arrow. Ru stopped and looked at where the arrow came from.

A woman stood at the edge of one of the watchtowers Pirouz had attacked. She held up a bow with another explosive arrow burning in the night. "Ru, stand down," she said. She jumped to where Ru, Xi, and Pirouz stood, right near the edge of the crater her arrow caused. The flame of her arrow went out. She slung her bow behind her back. "The girl is wearing the mask." The woman said.

"So what? How do we know that is *the* mask."

"I know it is because I know *the* mask. I have guarded it for most my life before that big oaf started wearing it."

"The one who killed Crimson Wolf is the one who has the mask." Pirouz thought Ru still sounded like a weasel.

"Yes, *she* did. That's what our intelligence report said."

"Why was I not told?"

"You did not need to know, Captain Ru. Stand down."

Ru lowered his weapon. "Everyone! Stand down!"

Xi raised her sword and ran at the woman. The woman unsheathed her blade, and the two traded a series of narrowly dodged death blows. "I WANT TO KILL ALL OF YOU!" Xi shouted, her vengeance still on her mind.

"I understand, young one." The woman said, gliding back towards a crowd of the Crimson Wolf guards. "And if you would like a death match with all of us, I can arrange that, but we must speak."

Xi put her twin sai up. "We have *nothing* to talk about!" Her scream was almost a cry. "NOTHING!"

The woman calmly put her blade up. "Xi... You will not survive if you go against me and you will never find out how I know your name. Rest, then, if you still want to kill us all after our chat, have at it. A young lady like you has better chances than most."

The scent of tea made the living quarters of the higher-ranking Crimson Wolves feel almost homey. Pirouz and Xi were sitting when a guard brought it out to them. The woman sat and spoke. "I appreciate you both calming yourselves." She pointed to Captain Ru, who stood by in the corner, on guard. "I understand you two know each other."

"Yes, yes, ma'am, he is an idiot." Pirouz saw Xi glare at him angrily. He shrugged for he did not have vengeance in his heart regarding the Crimson Wolves as Xi did.

The woman laughed. "It is funny hearing one speak of Captain Ru in such a disrespectful manner. He has cut out tongues for men saying far less."

"Yeah, well, he's an idiot."

She laughed. "You are a bold young man!"

"Thank you." Pirouz turned to look at Ru, he smiled, then looked back at the woman. "Did he ever tell you how he got that scar?"

Ru exploded. He broke from his guarding stance and shouted: "YOU SHUT YOUR FILTHY MOUTH!"

Pirouz jumped up to his feet and held his sword up. "COME HERE AND MAKE ME!"

The woman stood up between them. "Now now, gentlemen. *Do* be civil. You had your chance to slaughter each other; it has passed."

"You and your little girlfriend would have been dead if it wasn't for her."

"That's fine, I don't hide behind an army like you, coward."

The two were practically growling at one another, Xi sat and watched, hoping Pirouz would cut the man down. "Captain Ru, stand down." Captain Ru controlled his snarl when he looked at the woman, then bowed his head and stood back. "My name is Jia. What is yours? I know it but just to confirm."

"I will not share my name with a Crimson Wolf," Xi said, venom soaking her every word.

"I understand that. The blood feud between our clans has led to some misfortune."

"That's what you call killing my family?"

"What else would you like me to call it?"

Xi held up her twin sai. "Call it the reason you will die."

Jia smiled and let out a puff of air from her nostrils. "No, I don't think I will be doing that." She stood up. "The truth is, if you weren't wearing that mask birds would be eating your guts right now." She took a few steps with her hands behind her back, like she was pondering something. "Only the strongest of the strong, the mightiest of the mighty, can don the mask you wear."

"Yes, I killed a man for it and I will do it again!" Xi hissed.

"My foolish girl, do you not know what you have lucked into by donning that mask?"

"Not that I care, but what?"

Jia sat back down and stretched her hands out over the table where the teacups sat. "You now run the Crimson Wolf clan." She said this with a smile, Captain Ru's armor jangled as surprise burst across his face and the faces of the other guards.

"What are you talking about, crazy woman?"

"I can assure you, I am not crazy."

Pirouz noticed Ru glare at the lady when she said this, then look away. He spoke up. "Can I ask you a question?"

"Yes, please."

"Why do you even associate with such an idiot? Do you know how *mean* he is?"

"Permission to speak," Ru said.

"Speak," Replied Jia.

"Young man, I know not what your quarrel is with me." Pirouz tried to hide his disgust at the sound of Ru trying to appear peaceful. "I seem to have vague recollections of a young, simple boy in a school I attended but left."

"You were kicked out because of your cruelty, Ru. No amount of gold armor will hide your sadistic soul. If anything, the gold makes it shine brighter."

"Are we a poet now?" Ru chuckled, Jia smiled.

"I have a few verses I can share." Pirouz lowered his head so that he was looking at Ru from under his brow. "Want me to share some?" Pirouz put the handle of his sword up.

"No, I don't think he wants anything of the sort, for the sake of my mood." Jia looked at Xi. "Whoever wears the mask controls the Crimson Wolves. The wearer of the mask is chosen, by fate and blood spilled." Xi fell silent. Jia continued. "The *Crimson Wolf* was an arrogant buffoon who happened to have found the mask when our old leader died in the river during a gang battle between us and the Green Wolves." Jia's smile went away. "I can say this because he is dead now. He does not wear the mask; thus, he is unworthy of our praise."

"Wouldn't you want to honor his memory, like your stupid now dead master?"

"If you were anyone else, little girl… is all I will say." Xi felt how close to death she was when Jia said this; her cold stare could freeze wine.

"Now I wear the mask. Does that mean I hold a position over you?" Xi asked, calmer.

"Not until you make yourself available for a test, depending on whether you pass or not, then I will bow down to you."

"And if I refuse?"

"Either way, you have to fight for your life to get out of here, so what difference does it make?"

"Either way?" Xi asked. "Stop being so damn coy, tell me what you want of me?"

"You need to know something."

"What, damn you?"

"The killing of your family was simply a case of a bad decision made by old management." Jia held up her saber. "I have always been against the war between our clans. I always thought it was counterproductive to our cause."

"Your *cause*?" Xi repeated.

"Yes, *our* cause."

"What's your cause? You guys are two gangs, right?" Pirouz said this softly, trying not to offend.

"Our cause is survival by running the world of the shadows. You would know all about that, being a disciple of the House of Poison."

"I have no idea what you are talking about."

"Please. Our clan has always worked alongside the House. Our intelligence gathering is second to none. We knew you were coming here long before the boat was halfway across the ocean."

"Is that so?" Pirouz asked.

"Yeah. It is." Her eyes had an annoyed glare when she said this.

"Okay then. I admit nothing."

"Why the House of Poison sent a young student here, we can think of a few reasons. However, that is not a priority at the moment. What *is* a priority is letting you know that I personally had nothing to do with the death of your family. Everyone who did is dead now."

Moments later, Jia led them to the training yard. She told a story.

"Once there lived a little girl from a little village. This was long, long ago. Back when there were just tribes and bandits. This was also in a far-off land- unknown to most. Thought to be made up by others. I know it to be a true place, however, just from the things I have seen. This girl was the bravest child in her village. One day, bandits came and threatened to kill everyone if a tribute of their harvest was not given. The first night, they refused, so the bandits killed an entire family before saying they would return the next day, and if proper tribute was not given, everyone would be killed. Have you ever seen a shooting star or a rock fall from the sky?"

"No." Xi said.

"I have." Said Pirouz. "I saw a shooting star, a few times, actually."

Jia stopped in the center of the training ground. "In the story, the morning before the bandits came to claim their loot, the little girl prayed to a wolf goddess, whom the people worshipped."

"A wolf Goddess?" Pirouz asked, fascinated.

"Yes. As she was praying, a rock fell from the sky, nearly killing her. It was red and it glowed."

"Wow, that's neat," Pirouz said. Xi gave him an annoyed look.

Jia continued: "The rock had a red gel around it; it glowed like starfire. She took some of it and it quickly hardened and became so brittle it would turn to powder if she touched it. She decided to make a mask for the day she was to die, to protect her village. She mixed the red powder with water to paint the mask red, which was made from a fabric that people have tried to replicate for centuries. The combination of the specially textured fabric and the mysterious nature of dye created a mask that would mold itself to whoever wore it. The shape of their head, the furrow of their brow, etc. When the time came for the bandits to sweep the village and kill everyone, they were met with a little girl in a mask... She killed them all."

"Wow, that's a crazy story. Did the mask give her special abilities?"

"The mask gave her nothing she didn't already have, it simply brought out her gifts, it brought out the wolf warrior in all who wear it."

Xi touched the mask she was wearing. "Then what?" She asked.

"Then that little girl went on to become the fiercest warrior in the ancient world. She led a land to peace and prosperity through strong leadership." Jia smiled. "Would you be interested in knowing the relevance of this story to *you*?"

"That would be nice, yes," Xi said.

"You are wearing the mask from the story." She took a step toward Pirouz and Xi. "There is a high possibility you were chosen by fate to lead the Crimson Wolf Clan, for you wear the mask."

"Really?"

"*Maybe.*"

"Well, which is it?"

Ru stepped forward. "One of us has to kill each other. As the top captain, I have to administer the final test, which I have no doubt you will fail at. As much as I respect Madame Jia, I am not a believer in the power of the mask, if the previous fool could wear it and wreak havoc anyone can."

"I see, so we have to kill each other. Madame Jia, may I admire your blade?"

Madame Jia walked up Xi and held up her sword for her to see. "Do you care to hold it?" Jia asked.

"May I?" Xi said with a smirk. Pirouz could see that for the first time, Xi and Jia were smiling at one another. Jia handed her the sword. In a flash, the sword went from covered to blade out in Xi's hand. It flung from her hand just as quickly and stabbed itself directly into Captain Ru's face. Blood sprayed out like the blood of a recently decapitated lamb. The blood was bright red and momentarily clouded the air. Captain Ru's hands flailed up pathetically, as though he could reverse the damage, but it was too late. He hit the ground with the only movement being the blood pouring from his face. Xi walked over to the fresh corpse of the captain, put her foot over his head, and slid the sword out. "Sorry to bloody your blade. If that doesn't count, bring someone else over, and I will kill them just like this one. I could kill Crimson Wolves all day and wouldn't mind dying doing so." Pirouz chuckled when she said this.

"This counts," Jia said.

"So what now?" Xi asked.

Jia knelt down on one knee and bowed her head, then lifted her head up and stood. "I must teach you how we do things."

"So... what?"

"So you can begin to lead when you feel ready."

A week passed. Pirouz spent his time recovering from his wounds, as did Xi. He appreciated the fact that he was being allowed to recover on Crimson Wolf territory, though he bore no allegiance to them. On his last day, as he was drinking tea on the bridge, Jia approached him. "I wish we could protect you on the rest of your journey, young friend, but the rest of this mountain is known to be deadly beyond our control."

"That's fine," Pirouz said, looking out at the roaring river below. "I did not count on your help when I came to the island. Or Xi's, for that matter. I thought when I got here I could go at it alone."

"No one can *go at it* alone. Everyone needs people. Some form families, others form whole groups. We Crimson Wolves know that. I am sure with your teachers, you sense that."

"I suppose so." Pirouz looked serious. "I have to find out who killed master... and I must avenge him." He looked at Jia and smiled. "Otherwise, I would love to stay..." He paused. The river sounds filled in the silence.

Jia said, after a few moments, "If you die on the rest of your journey, my only hope is that it is not painful."

"Hey, me too!" Pirouz said with a goofy smile. Jia chuckled and went to go speak to Xi, who was in her living quarters, to teach her more about leading the Crimson Wolves.

It was when Pirouz was leaving that Xi walked with him part of the way, a bit of distance from camp. "If you're ever in need of Crimson Wolf protection, now you got a hookup!" Xi said with a smile. Her rage had simmered down, and she was getting used to the idea of running an entire clan.

"Thanks Xi, hopefully I won't but you never know with life. By the way, so you're gonna leave the mask on?" Pirouz had in fact not seen Xi without the mask since they got to the village.

"You know what's funny? I just don't want to." She touched

the mask as they walked. "It's really comfortable."

Pirouz stopped where a trail began. "You said we'd split here. Here we are."

"Yeah." Xi sounded slightly melancholic when she said this.

"Xi... it would be nice to stick around with you, but..."

"You have some vengeance to get to, I get it."

"Yeah." He snapped his fingers. "We may catch each other on the way down, though?"

"Will you? You'll stop through?"

"Definitely. I can take a break for a day or two if you don't mind, my vengeance may exhaust me!"

"That would be good..." She had a smile on, but it faded. "If you get killed, I'll send the wolves to go find who did it and kill them."

"I appreciate that, Xi, but you don't have to say that. I'm not worth any of the lives of your men, and you know what they say about the rest of the mountain."

"Yeah, I do... if I don't see you again..." She gave her head a slight bow of respect. "it was nice meeting you."

Pirouz, too, gave his head a slight bow of respect. "Yes, it was nice meeting you as well."

The last piece of Crimson Wolf territory was the Emerald Mines. Pirouz approached the foreman who oversaw the entrance with great respect. He showed him a medallion that Jia had given him to show so that he could pass through peacefully and get something to eat at the mine workers' tavern. The foreman gave Pirouz a cold look, then looked at the medallion for a moment. He looked back at Pirouz, and his stare became less cold. "The tavern is just past the caves. Show them what you showed me, and they'll get you anything they have to eat and drink."

"Thank you, sir." Pirouz gave a bow of respect with his fist slapped against his palm. The foreman just nodded his head. Pirouz noticed men, all of them in the Crimson Wolf clan fabrics like those in the previous village, only these men were all dusted with the pulverized rocks they were rummaging through through to find stones. He noticed a group of men comparing purple stones that shone a certain way as the sun was going down, basking everything in pink light. Pirouz was able to find the tavern with no problem at all. He noticed the workers were all too exhausted to pay much mind to him, which he liked.

The tavern was half full of Crimson Wolf miners, all of them with their pickaxes at their sides and their drinks in front of them. They all had the same sunbaked, tired look, nothing like the soldiers in the village who all seemed ready to kill on command. "Hello, may I have some wine, please?" Pirouz asked, showing the man behind the counter the medallion. The man, a bald gentleman, gave a nod of respect and poured him a cup of wine.

Pirouz did not usually drink wine, but the fact of the matter was he found himself feeling sentimental. *I hope I see Xi again,* he thought. He drank his wine quietly, then decided to have some of the stew that the place offered. He let the stew cool down, thinking of returning the scarf to Crystal Sparrow as it did. He finished his cup of wine and asked for some more. "If you don't mind me asking..." Pirouz turned to his side to see where the voice was coming from. A man with a cut face and a youthful glare in his eyes was sitting, staring straight ahead of him. "Why are you looking so glum, young man?"

"Who, me?" Pirouz said.

"You're the only young man here."

Pirouz looked around. "Are you sure about that?"

"These are all men well older than you. The Wolves don't have the young ones working the mines." Pirouz looked around. He realized the men could have all been either 25 or 60 years old; they were so caked in dirt it was difficult to tell. "These men don't have your spirit. Most of them-not all and not me certainly-are quite dead inside."

"I've heard this happens with some people." Pirouz sipped some more wine.

"You keep drowning your sorrows; it just may happen... if

you're not careful."

Pirouz sipped some more. "I'll be careful then."

"I am happy to hear this, you're far too young to mope about drunk."

"Yeah, I like to mope about sober."

"If that is how you enjoy passing your time, who am I to judge?"

"I don't mope to pass the time... It's just when I was a boy, my master accused me of being mopey."

"Really?"

"Yeah, that's why I like to be as happy as I can be. He used to tell me there was nothing worse than being a mope."

"With respect to your master, I think there *are* worse things than being a mope." He smiled. "Being sad is just resisting what is, sometimes, with some people."

"You don't get sad?"

"I am a human. Of course I get sad. I feel whatever I need to be feeling. I find it is best to be malleable, like water, my friend."

"That's a nice philosophy." Pirouz let out a sigh. "I am going to be heading up Demon's Peak. Is there anything you know of that region? Who guards it at the moment?"

"The man who stands at the top of Demon's Peak is an old man, a foreigner, they call him *The Skull Crusher*."

"Do they call him that because he crushes skulls?"

"I know they don't call him that because he makes good soup, that's for sure."

"*Does* he make good soup?"

There was a pause, then the man said: "No." He looked away from Pirouz to the back of the bar. "The Skull Crusher was a mercenary before he came to the island. He tends to work for bandits when he's not here."

"Why is he here?" Pirouz asked.

"Because he wants to crush the skulls of the biggest and best in the world, and what better place to do that than on Murder Mountain, my friend." A warm smile spread across his face. "I would love to see you try to defeat him."

"And why is that?"

"Because I have been writing his story for what seems like forever, and I am looking forward to it ending."

"Is that your business?"

"Yes, as a matter of fact it is." He turned to face Pirouz. "I am a chronicler of the lives of heroes and villains of the martial world."

"Wow, really? Who have you covered?"

"I've chronicled a bunch of Crimson Wolves, I did all of the members of the House of Poison, and pretty much most of the guys and gals here, and that's it." Pirouz could tell, the way the man mentioned the House of Poison, that the man knew nothing of Pirouz's affiliation. "Hey, if you defeat the Skull Crusher, I'll chronicle you!" His smile got bigger. "Can I show you my finest work?"

"Sure."

The man pulled up a leather bag and pulled out a piece of parchment with a figure in various stages of life, fighting, with calligraphy printed in the blackest of ink. "Have you ever heard of Míngzé, from the House of Poison?"

"I can't say that I have. I've heard of the House of Poison but only as a rumor." He took a closer look at the parchment. "That's wonderful work."

"Thank you!" He chuckled. "I have one I did on the warrior Ice Snake and his ongoing adventures."

"Oh. How does it end?"

"It ends triumphantly with the battle of a thousand men!" He put his hands up. "I know, I know, that story has been embellished through time, but I feel I did a good depiction of it."

"I am sorry to say this, sir, but Ice Snake recently met his demise."

"What? Surely you are joking."

"I am afraid I am not. I was there." The man looked heartbroken and still. "What is your name, sir?"

"I am Níng."

"Well, Níng, I am Pirouz. It's nice to meet you."

"Yes, yes, likewise." He looked at Pirouz after looking off

into space for a moment. "How did he die?"

Pirouz explained the story of the hunter and the *hunters* and the old man and the snow things in the Garden of Eternal Winter. Níng listened to every detail with his mouth slightly open, in awe. By the end of it, Pirouz went on to detail Xi and the Crimson Wolves and her becoming their leader in training under the tutelage of Madame Jia.

"That is truly all amazing. I am deeply saddened by the death of Ice Snake. Like many I heard of his stories since I was a young boy, but all of this you tell me, of your friend Xi avenging the Green Wolves only to become the leader of the Crimsons, is truly a shocking turn of events."

"Yeah, it's been a lot." Pirouz had to ask: "How are you here? You're not a mine worker. They don't seem like the type of people to let you just hang around."

"The Crimson Wolves are big fans of my work and want nothing more than for me to chronicle the grand story of *them*. Thus, they give me unlimited access. The same access you have with that medallion."

"Is the Skull Crusher a big guy?"

"Yeah, usually guys with names of that nature are big."

Pirouz and Níng decided to travel with one another towards Demon's Peak, where the Skull Crusher was known to stand waiting for a skull to crush. Níng explained that he was trying to make it up the mountain simply to chronicle his experience. They left the Crimson Wolf mines after eating a large meal and reached the rocky terrain that led up to Demon's Peak. They crawled over the rocks in a jagged way as they spoke.

"You're awfully brave to come to Murder Mountain just to chronicle people."

"Everyone needs a reason to die, I feel. Mine is to chronicle the lives of martial heroes."

"That sounds like a reason to *live*."

"You know what I mean. I would risk my life to hear a good story. To be able to repeat it to people, in my own words, is beautiful and, honestly, difficult to explain. I just love it."

"That's nice I suppose." Pirouz found the man's enthusiasm to be both charming and strange. A sudden blast of smoke burst before them, the smoke was cleared by the wind, revealing four men clad in black and purple with their faces covered. The one closest to Pirouz and Níng spoke:

"We are the Knuckles of the Skull Crusher!"

"*The Knuckles*? What do you mean?"

"The Skull Crusher is a deity of combat, and we are his students! You are not worthy of his time, so we are here to kill you!"

"Come here and get some." Pirouz said, his hand up, welcoming them over. The men all did flips in the air in unison and landed in front of Pirouz. They were slashed down by Pirouz's blade, their limbs still holding their swords when they splattered down to the rocks.

"You are quite good with that sword," Níng said, examining the screaming men on the rocks, one of them holding his own arm.

"I'm just not in the mood to dilly-dally." He sheathed his sword. "Let's go."

The two began walking further up the rocks. "There will be more little knuckles here and there, I imagine." The second the word left Níng's lips, another *knuckle*, clad in a charcoal grey face mask, jumped out from behind a large boulder and landed in front of Níng. Níng leapt back, then forward and unleashed a skillful series of blows to the man's chest, then kicked him in that very spot, knocking him off his feet and sending his back crashing down on the jagged rocks.

"You're trained?" Pirouz asked as they kept walking.

"Yeah, a little. My father trained me. I enjoy it, but I enjoy documenting it more; otherwise, all of these stories will just vanish like dust in the wind."

"Everything will." Pirouz said darkly. A gloom had enveloped his heart since parting with Xi.

"Yes, but that is just outlook, my friend. Everything is what you make of it. There is always a bright side and downside."

They walked further up the rocks. They could see the man sitting alone at the top of the mountain. He looked like a bulky lump from afar. "Does he expect us to go to *him*?"

"Well, yeah. You don't get to the top of this pile of rocks to go down and greet people."

They reached the flat piece of rock where the Skull Crusher sat. Pirouz shouted: "Skull Crusher. I am Pirouz. Allow me to pass, I see what is at the top of this mountain."

"Young man." The Skull Crusher grumbled; one eye opening. "I am protecting you by not letting you pass." Both eyes opened. "Beyond this point, the mountain becomes *Diyu.*"

Pirouz would not have admitted it, but a shiver went shimmering through his bones. He had long feared the afterlife world of *Diyu,* where the 12,800 hells awaited the wicked. "Sir, if you are truly protecting me, I appreciate it, but I must pass."

"I am called the Skull Crusher because I have even crushed the skull of my own son for disobeying me."

"I see. That is some very strict parenting, I would say." Pirouz looked at Níng and asked softly. "That's true?"

"Yes according to legend and now according to him, yes." Níng raised his hand. "Hello Skull Crusher, I have documented your life! I am here looking for a story."

"I shall crush your skull as well. Documenting my life makes no difference to me." He coughed, sounding like he hacked up a bucket of phlegm, then spit. "I am in no rush, however. Please, if you care to, sit before I crush your skull."

"Very well, sir." Pirouz looked at Níng. "Do you have a problem with that?"

"No, not at all. Why rush into things?" Pirouz and Níng sat on the ground, Pirouz stretched his legs out.

"Thank you, I need a second to rest." He said.

"Yes, I'm impressed someone your size has come this far." He sniffed the air. "You both have candied fruit on you. May I have some?" Pirouz and Níng looked at one another, then at the Skull Crusher and nodded their heads. They both did in fact have candied fruit on them, and so, Pirouz offered a few pieces, as did Níng, by cautiously presenting their bag to him. Skull Crusher carefully picked the cherries from each bag, then grumbled, "Thank you." They sat back down. Skull Crusher put one of the cherries in his mouth and started chewing. "It's good," he said.

"Yes. Cherries are your favorite?"

"Yes." He replied, his voice sounding like it had rocks in it. "Why do you seek to go further, young man? Is it for fame in the martial world?"

"I don't care about fame in the martial world. I want something that's at the top and I want to kill the man who killed my master."

"Ah. Revenge."

"Yeah, I suppose so."

"As impressive as your survival up until now has been, nothing can prepare you for what is on the other side, thus it is more likely that you will die under my hand. I cannot imagine why the fates would let you go beyond this point, for you shall surely die before the moon moves but a hair."

"Yeah? Why do you say that, Skull Crusher? What's so big and scary that isn't some guy who is skilled or some hairy monster with spooky eyes? I've seen it all so far."

"This mountain holds a secret. I am the keeper of that secret. It is the reason I wait here to crush skulls."

"Instead of being cryptic, you can just tell me. What difference does it make if you're so sure you're gonna crush my skull?"

"You are right." He smiled. "The Hell Dragon kills all."

Chapter 8:
Hell Dragon

"The Hell Dragon?" Pirouz said. "I've studied everything everyone has ever told me about this island and this mountain, I have never heard of the Hell Dragon."

"That is because the Hell Dragon is holy."

"Really?" Pirouz's patience with the old, dusty man was beginning to wear thin. "Tell me about the Hell Dragon."

"It comes from Diyu, from all 12,800 hells. He is in fact the architect of them."

"*Really?*" Pirouz chuckled. "So, a *Hell Dragon*, who built the 12,800 hells of Diya just hangs out on that side of the mountain, ey? Is this a little dragon? How come no one has seen it?"

"He is in fact quite large."

"Right, so, answer my question, how come no one has seen it?"

There was a pause, then another grumble: "He hides."

"I see." Pirouz raised his eyebrow at Níng.

"Sir, I have also been chronicling all of the island, and I have not heard of the Hell Dragon."

"You see, I am humoring you two. I am amused to see such small beings get this far up the mountain. I have killed anyone who has come here, no one has gone further."

"How long has the Hell Dragon been here?"

"Since the hole to the diya opened, just beyond these rocks."

"Are you his assistant or something like that?" Pirouz kept his hand firmly gripped on the handle of his sword.

"I am just a man smart enough to recognize the only deity that matters."

"You *could* be crazy." Pirouz said, Níng sent him a worried look. "Maybe the dragon is just in your head, have you thought of that?"

Skull Crusher plucked one of the torches next to him out

of the ground, then threw it behind him. The firelight revealed a mountain of skulls. "Notice these skulls are not crushed."

Níng whistled, Pirouz just stared on, shocked, and said to himself: "That's a lot of dead."

"I tire of speaking to you." He got up, dust clouded off him. He removed the blanket that covered him, his arms were bulging with muscles and looked to be the size of wine kegs. He had metal plates on his knuckles, which cracked when he pressed down on them with his thumbs. *RAAAAA* was the sound he made when he barreled forward. Pirouz's sword was out the second he started running. The moment the two warriors met, the blade met the steel plates on his knuckles over and over until Níng flipped in the air, landing in front of the two. Skull Crusher swung his fist in Níng's direction, who dodged a swing that would have taken his head off had Skull Crusher not missed. Níng sent him a kick in the ribs, which made a loud crack. Skull Crusher barely moved and smashed down in front of him, causing an explosion in the rocks that careened Pirouz and Níng into the air. Pirouz landed on his knees, tumbling away in a dust rock cloud. Níng's back hit a boulder, causing him to fall flat on his chest and face. Pirouz got up to his feet. He looked at Níng, who jumped upward without his hands touching the ground. He cracked his neck, put his hands up, and let out a cat-like howl. He then made a series of more howls as he punched the air toward the Skull Crusher, then jumped and landed a kick into Skull Crusher's face. Skull Crusher flung Níng away. He hit more rocks. Pirouz, sword up, flew toward Skull Crusher and smashed his sword repeatedly on the metal plates on Skull Crusher's hands. The sparks lit up the night. Pirouz was smashing the sword so hard and fast, he was floating just over Skull Crusher's fists.

Finally, Pirouz hit the ground a small distance away from Skull Crusher, who was holding his hands up. They were smoldering with smoke. "You are an annoying one." He said.

"I've been told that." Pirouz said. Níng was back on his feet, in his fighting stance, making another cat howl. "Who's more annoying, him or me?"

"You are both equally annoying."

"What if this were a contest?" Pirouz asked.

"You, most definitely."

"Thank you that makes me happy." Pirouz zipped up to Skull Crusher yet again, the two reigniting a lightning storm of hits that all blurred together. Skull Crusher smashed his fists into one another, the force of which caused a shockwave in the air that vibrated through Pirouz's sword while he flew back into the same boulder Níng slammed into earlier. Níng performed a tizzy of punches, dodging the massive fists of the Skull Crusher at every turn. Pirouz was back on his feet, dashing the action with sword up. The Skull Crusher pumped both fists. Pirouz could see the darts shoot out of the metal plates on his knuckles, he deflected all four of them, making *ting* sounds in rapid succession. "You want to play like that, ey?" Pirouz took the first needle he could reach for on his belt and threw it at the Skull Crusher. The needle landed right between his eyes.

"Annoying little bastard." He growled. The veins began to bulge from his skin. At first, the color of the veins were that of the rest of his face. They quickly went from green to purple as they bulged around his head and face. The blood first sprayed out of his nose and mouth. Then his eyes inflated and turned pink, then deep red, then they looked like two cherries exploding into a rouge juice. His eye sockets became bloody fountains once the initial explosion of red occurred. The blood flowed down his swollen face, which went from white to pink to purple; the poison from the tip of the needle had done its work. Even though the blood continued to flow out of his eyes, his face continued to swell up and turn purple and pink. His gravelly voice began to sound like he was gargling blood. It quickly became evident that he *was* gargling blood, as streams of blood slid down his chin and spotted the air. A geyser of the red stuff spewed from his mouth after the initial stream. His face bulged further, making him almost featureless, like the heads of three or four swollen mushrooms, squeezed together. The Skull Crusher's head then fully exploded. A thin stream of his blood squirted upwards from the wound on his neck, and he slumped forward, cracking against the rocks.

Pirouz dusted himself off, staring at the body. Níng got blood on his face from the head explosion. "What a way to tell someone you're from the House of Poison."

"I don't know what you're talking about."

"Oh please." He scooped off a bit of brain from near his eye and flung it off his hand. "Firstly, your fighting technique is a dead giveaway. Secondly, there are only a few people in the martial world that can throw a needle the way you did. Most of these people are in the House of Poison. Thirdly, I have seen that poison before, the kind that makes your head explode. I believe it is called *Exploding Head Poison*, and the only time I saw it used was by was the great Master Míngzé."

"What else do you know?"

"I know that House of Poison members are sworn to secrecy." He wiped the blood off his hands with the cloth of his clothing. "I have heard, from various people, that in the very chapter that Míngzé trained and worked and ran things, there was a little foreign prince who was allowed to train with them... I also heard a rumor that is yet to be confirmed... that Míngzé is dead."

Pirouz, knowing it was best not to outright confirm what Níng was saying, simply responded with: "Your sources seem very reliable... Let's go." Pirouz started walking. He jumped over Skull Crusher's body, towards the mountain of skulls. He noticed Níng was still standing where the fight occurred. He stopped to look at him. From the way he was standing and the look on his face, it was clear he would not be coming with Pirouz. Pirouz walked back. "You're not coming, are you?"

Níng looked embarrassed. "I would... if I wanted to die." He looked at the mountain of skulls behind Pirouz, then looked back at him. "It just seems like certain death, and if I die, I cannot tell stories."

"I understand, sir. Thank you for helping me fight Skull Crusher."

Pirouz was about to walk away when Níng stopped him

with a question: "Why do you want to die?"

"I don't."

"To go any further is suicide, my young friend."

"There is something I have to do, if I die attempting it, that is my fate. I've accepted this fact, but I cannot rest until I know I have done all I can to do what I need to do."

"In that case, my young friend... if the stories of the young foreign prince are true, and Master Míngzé is dead... I hope he finds who did it."

Pirouz simply nodded his head and walked away, towards the mountain of skulls. He turned the corner past a mountain of skulls, then stayed there for what seemed like an eternity, terrified. He could hear a roaring fire off in the distance. *This will probably be the thing that kills you*, Pirouz thought. He thought, for a moment, as the fires raged beyond the mountain of bones, how odd it was that there even would be such a thing called a *Hell Dragon*. It was thought, in his world, that dragons were bringers of great luck. He did, however, once hear from Míngzé, that there were other dragons in the world... dragons of a bloodthirsty nature.

"Hello boy." Pirouz heard a sweet but sinister voice say this in a whisper. Like the person was in his ear. He turned around, startled, and saw, sitting far up on the mountain of bones, a woman with her legs crossed. Her back was arched forward and her hair, long and stringy and black, fell before her face which had a crooked smile on it. "You've come a long way."

"Hello," Pirouz said, backing up from the mountain of bones. "I am simply passing through."

She laughed, a quiet giggle. "People don't come here to pass through."

"What do they come here to do?"

She looked around at the skulls she was sitting on. "I am sitting on the bones of thousands of dead people, what do you *think* they come here to do? They come here to die!"

"Is that why you're here?"

"No... I am dead *inside* already." She laughed. "I'm just

joking." She hissed: "I'm *alive!*" She got up quickly and raced down the mountain of bones, the skulls around her doing a mini avalanche down. She reached Pirouz, who tried to back away without appearing too frightened. "So why do you wanna die?"

"What?"

"You just walked over here, you *obviously* are suicidal or something, that's great. Why though? I'm curious."

"I don't want to die."

"Are you sure? At this moment you're standing near mountains of bones that you can see from far away. Why else would you be here?"

"I have a task I have to perform."

"Oh, you're one of those." She looked around at all the skulls. "Or one of *these*, I should say." She wagged her finger at him. "You know, you seem like a good kid. I will offer to kill you for nothing, just let me have all that stuff you got on you."

"No, thank you,"

"Okay,"

"I think I should be going," Pirouz started walking. The woman trailed along, skipping like a child. "Do you have some sort of disease or something?"

"No, not to my knowledge."

"Okay, just checking. I don't care if you do. I'll still kill you if you want."

"I don't want you to kill me." Pirouz was getting annoyed.

"Okay, last chance!"

"If I change my mind I'll let you know."

As Pirouz walked up the hill on the side of Murder Mountain, which had mountains of bones scattered across it, he could finally begin to see the edge of a surface. The fire that was burning off in the distance, filling the night air with its furious sound, seemed to be going just beyond where Pirouz could see. He did not want to know the answer to the question he was about to ask, but he *had* to know. "Why are *you* here?"

"I'm a witch." She smiled. "You are so lucky."

"Why am I lucky?"

"Because you're here!"

"Funny, this place does not seem like one of good fortune."

"It *could* be. The Hell Dragon brings forth wonderful things."

"Like bones?"

"No," she put her hand up, then noticed something behind Pirouz. "Look!"

Pirouz looked behind him. A large, rotund man was racing down the mountain of bones, holding a golden box. Another man was racing behind him.

The witch giggled. "They're cousins!" The man chasing after the large man with the box wore some sort of cloth that looked to be made of gold. Both men were bleeding at the face and knuckles. The man with the box stopped and put the box on top of a skull, then pumped his fists up into a sloppy fighting stance, yelled warrior-like, and then ran toward the oncoming golden-clothed man. The chubby man got the first hit in, slamming his fat fist against the golden man's face, causing a smack and crack that Pirouz and the Witch could hear even over the fires from beyond. Golden man clawed at his opponent's face, scratching and ripping the skin, leaving a red trail that began to stream blood. Both men fell to the bones below, wrestling as the man with the golden clothes dug his fingers deeper into the man with the golden box's skin.

The witch laughed as the golden-clothed man's fingers wiggled their way into the other man's eye socket, squishing his eye out of his head. He plucked his finger out of the eye hole and then grabbed the nearest skull and proceeded to pound the skull into his opponent's, smashing it until the man's head was nothing but bones and a fine red and pink pulp. He gasped. Pirouz looked at the Witch, who had a big smile across her face, then back at the bloody aftermath of the fight. The victor of the fray got up and dropped the bloody skull, which plopped to the ground. He then dropped to his knees and put his head down, as though in shame. Pirouz stood there and watched with the witch as the man pulled a golden dagger from his clothing and stabbed himself in the throat. He ripped it out, letting out a squirting of cherry red. He then slumped forward and died.

"What was that all about?"

"That was just a good show!" She said enthusiastically.

"Did you know those guys?"

"I saw them come through. Like most people here, they wanted all of the gold! And so Hell Dragon gave it to them, then it tore them apart! Then they joined the sad ocean of bones." She mocked a sad face and rubbed her finger against each other near her eyes, mimicking tears.

"At least they got the gold." Pirouz said with a sarcastic shrug.

"The Hell Dragon gives you what you want, you see? It just so happens it makes everyone lose their mind!" She laughed. "Or it will have forever horrible consequences."

"So why do people come here then?"

"Good old-fashioned greed, little boy."

"Why are *you* here?"

"I like the show."

Pirouz looked away from the two dead bodies and sat down, trying to gather his thoughts. "But the dragon still kills as well, right?"

"Yes, he can be very prickly. Sometimes he wants to see the instant effects of violence his magic has; other times, he just incinerates people. I would say it's about half and half."

"Have you been beyond here? To the temple at the top?"

"Only a few people have." She made a face. "I think the ones that have are still there. The Hell Dragon is a secret of the island. Most of the fighters that have come here hear about it in the village then go through the back way."

"*The back way?*"

"Yes, it's just on the other side of the mountain. They would go to avoid the Skull Crusher and the Crimson Wolves. They would come here and then the Hell Dragon would use them for entertainment."

Pirouz gave her a puzzled look. "How have you survived here?"

"You don't want to know, boy." She got up. "If you want to make it past the Hell Dragon, I can take you to a bone tunnel, but then you would have to deal with hell creatures from the 128,000 hells."

"That's a tough choice." He sighed. "What if I don't want anything from the Hell Dragon?"

"You don't want *anything*?"

"No, not if it means me ending up like *those* guys. Besides, if someone is surrounded by all these bones, why would they even trust the Hell Dragon?"

"Oh, silly boy, because he infects the mind. But not mine!"

"You're just here because you're thinking straight?"

"You watch it, little boy. I am a kind witch, but that can all change according to my mood."

"Sorry."

"That's okay. I will tell you." She looked up. "When I grew up, I noticed some people did not see a lot of blood from their parents and people around them. I did, though. So I heard about dragons- all kinds -and I became obsessed with them. I found a few in my time, but this one is the one that I find the most beautiful. He is not good, he is not bad. He simply is, something that is big and beautiful and natural and unnatural at the same time. If he wanted to, he could annihilate the world or heal it. When he grants a wish, and that person gets what they want, he reveals the true nature of man, because it always becomes their undoing. He shows that human beings are murderous and, whether they know it or not, suicidal. We can't help but kill ourselves and those around us, and that is why I love the Hell Dragon."

Pirouz simply gave this a nod. He heard a voice that sounded like the voices of a thousand men rumble from the sky: "Bring the prince to me."

The witch's eyes enlarged and darted toward Pirouz. "Ahhh, is that you?"

"Was that...?" The hairs on Pirouz's neck were standing up.

"Yes... Hell Dragon."

"I would rather not go, on second thought."

"But the Hell Dragon wants you!"

"I'll go on my own time, thank you."

"I don't think so." She put her fingers to her lips and whistled. The skeletons that were not crushed began to move and shake all at once, tumbling towards one another, forming an army of skeletons within a matter of a few grains of sand passing through an hourglass. Pirouz was surrounded; the dead army was armed as well, with the swords of the fallen. *These are different from the jiangshi,* Pirouz thought. He quickly noticed some of them still had half-decomposed flesh sticking to the bones. He could even see some with eyeballs. He swung his sword at the first wave of them. Being dead, many of them were frail and tumbled over one another at the contact of the blade. More bone soldiers attacked Pirouz, but he kept his own, slamming his sword through them, splintering the skeletons like wood.

The witch laughed while Pirouz pounded through each wave of the skull army, reducing each member to mere fragments, ten soldiers at a time. He was tiring quickly, but he kept on smashing. After the last bone warrior was destroyed by a mighty smash to the head, Pirouz slammed his sword into the ground to catch his breath. He was panting with his head down, exhausted, when he heard the Witch shout: "Look around you, boy, you're surrounded by my army. Either come with us or die resisting.

"No," Pirouz muttered under his breath. She could sense what he said.

"Damn you!" She clapped her hands together and shut her eyes. "You will feel the wrath of my army of death!" She nodded her head. A green light blasted from her forehead, flooding the surrounding bone yard, then disappeared. As quickly as several strikes of lightning, a new army of skeletons was fully assembled, ready to destroy Pirouz. "Get him!" the witch shouted.

Pirouz moved backwards, as behind him there were now moving skeletons as far as he could sense. He kept moving, slicing at the oncoming skeletons and blue-skinned dead people with the ferocity of a human tornado. With each step backward, the onslaught looked to be thicker and thicker, until behind him it looked like a wave of bones was cascading toward him. His back was now up against one of the large boulders up the hill. He climbed up it. The skeletons, which from afar must have looked like a swarm of white insects, were advancing at an increasing rate. Pirouz found himself rushing up the hill then rolling over the edge, to the flat surface of the hilltop.

As he got up, he noticed nothing but red rocks in front of him. He thought to climb them, but then thought better of it, as they looked steaming red hot. They moved suddenly, then separated at the middle, revealing what looked like a large ball of orange and black glass with a sliver down the middle. The sliver moved, causing Pirouz to jump. He was staring into the eye of the dragon. The eye moved back, showing itself to belong to a fearsome beast of red and black with eyes that burned bright and red. Its skin looked like it was made from the boulders of the mountain as if they were dipped in red paint. The neck was long, like that of a gargantuan lizard. It seemed to have four legs in total- one set near the head, the other near the tail.

"I see the boy has finally arrived."

Pirouz could hear the clunking sound of the skeleton army carrying the witch over to where he stood, then clunk back down the hill, disappearing. "Yes, as you can see he did not want to come, so the bones had to convince him."

"I am Pirouz, son of King Yazdegerd."

"I know who you are, idiot." The dragon sounded annoyed. "And from what I understand, your father being king was heavily debated."

"What?! How dare you say such a thing!" Pirouz thought, dragon or not, my father's name will not be disrespected.

"I dare say it. Boy, in some areas of your region, he did not even have coins minted. Now what kind of king would you call that?"

"My father was a king, you're just being provocative."

"Your father was killed for next to nothing by a lowly grain miller."

"Yes, I know, I was there."

"So was I."

"I don't remember you being there."

"I was there in spirit, I suppose."

"Let me pass."

"Why would you like to pass?"

"I want to retrieve the Savior Sword and find the one who killed my master."

"Aaaah." The dragon smiled. "The one who killed your master," His serpent-like neck curled and twisted as his head raised high up in the sky. "I understand the ones responsible for killing your father met with gruesome ends, no?"

"Yes, that is what I am told."

"Tortured to death, from what I understand."

"Yes, something like that."

"Persian politics can be quite harsh." His eyes narrowed and his mouth twisted into a smile. "It must be difficult being you... you must feel your very existence is pointless."

"I don't... no."

The dragon growled, "Then why are you on this mountain?"

"I told you why."

"No, there is a true reason. You want to die."

"Everyone says that. I *don't* want to die."

"Your very own masters told you before you came on this trip, did they not?"

"They said it was suicidal to do what I am doing, but that is not why I do what I do."

"Do you feel it simmering within you as you speak to me?"

"Feel what?"

The dragon smiled, his teeth shone in the glare of the night fire. "Rage."

Pirouz was silent. He no longer wished to engage. "Let me pass."

"Feel free," the dragon said nonchalantly. He brought his

head close to Pirouz, who took several steps back, nearly tripping. "You could, however, use my infinite wisdom and power to accomplish your goals."

"How so?"

"Well, I happen to know who killed your master."

Pirouz gripped his sword in anger. "You do?"

"Of course I do, I know all."

"Well please, tell me."

The dragon laughed. "Foolish boy, I want something in return."

"Yeah? What would that be?"

"I want you to do what you are good at," the dragon's head lifted back up into the air. "I want you to kill a man." His eye glowed and a flame flared from his mouth and nostrils.

"*You* want me to kill a man? I think you would have no problem doing it yourself."

"He is in an area of the mountain I do not wish to go to, he is a shaman."

"Is he in one of the monasteries here?"

"No, not at all. He lives in a humble little shack."

Pirouz looked puzzled. "May I ask why you, a dragon, would want me to kill a man?"

"Not that it is any of your business…" the dragon began to coil. "But he has been trying to expel the mountain of me. He feels I do not belong in this world. He put a spell on himself so I cannot come near him."

"Okay."

"Okay?" The dragon raised his left brow.

"Okay. Tell me where he is."

"He is just up the mountain. I can take you a bit away from his lowly shack. He is a lowly man."

"Anything I should know about him?"

"He carries extra weight."

Pirouz took this as meaning the man was heavy. The dragon brought his head down, offering his neck up for Pirouz to ride. Pirouz took a breath, then hopped up on the dragon's back. Before he knew it, the dragon was speeding through the air. He looked behind him, noticing, getting smaller and smaller, the witch waving goodbye with a crooked smile on her face and her eyes big like two coins. The dragon, as though showing off, flew up high into the sky, above the mountain. Pirouz's stomach felt like it dropped as he looked down below, the mountain could now be seen, surrounded by the ocean which sparkled in the moonlight. The dragon swooped back down, going down in a spiral motion. Pirouz held onto the creature's red mane like fur, afraid to let go out of fear of plummeting to his death. Just as he thought that he would like the dragon to slow down, the beast went faster, like an arrow that was the size of a temple.

Pirouz closed his eyes before he hit the ground, as they were going so fast he was sure, in that moment, that he was going to die by hitting the dirt. Instead, the Hell Dragon gently floated above the grass where they were, which looked like it was on the other side of the mountain, far above and away from the hellfire of the hell dragon. "Get off." Pirouz hopped off, then collapsed to his knees from the dizziness. "The Shaman lives in that stone hut." Pirouz was not looking; he was on his hands now, staring at the grass with a queasy feeling in his stomach. "Hey, are you listening to me?"

"Yes, he lives in that stone hut." Pirouz got up, then hunched over and threw up. The dragon flowed out in front of him. "You need a decent meal. Here." Pirouz opened his eyes to see an entire feast before him. Steamed vegetables and various plates of sea food like lobster and fish and a whole roast chicken along with a jug with what looked like wine. "You should eat and sleep. Let your stomach settle with some good food." Pirouz gave the dragon a suspicious look. The dragon took this in, then said, "I have every reason for you to want to be healthy because I want this shaman dead. So trust me, the food is safe. Just eat it or die because you were too weak and tired to fight."

Pirouz sat down in the grass, in front of the food, and started to eat. He picked up the chicken with both hands and bit into it. It was still hot, but not so hot that it would scald his tongue. He put it down and picked up the jug of wine and took in a mighty gulp of it, then put that down and started helping himself to a plate of fresh oysters. "Thank you." He said.

"You're welcome." The dragon looked at the stone hut. It was far enough away, and there were enough trees spotted along the hill on the side of the mountain that Pirouz and he could not be seen. "I will be happy when this is done."

"Do you mind giving more details about all this?"

"Sure." The dragon said. "He summoned me."

Pirouz's mouth was full of chicken as he chewed and said, "He summoned you?"

"Yes. I was not always here; this has been very recent. That is why you didn't know about me, you bastard."

"Don't be mad that I didn't know you."

"Whatever. Once you kill him, the spell will be broken, and I can get off of this horrible island."

"Oh, so you are stuck here."

"Slice this idiot's throat and I won't be."

Pirouz bit into a whole piece of grilled fish, right at the belly where most of the meat but little of the bones were. He then said, spitting out white chunks of fish meat: "So is this guy the boss of you because he summoned you?"

"You are playing a dangerous game when you taunt a being that can burn you to a crisp in a heartbeat."

"I guess I am, sorry, I feel a little delirious."

"Yes, you have not slept. You should sleep."

"You don't want me to kill your guy?"

"You can get to it in the morning." The Hell Dragon blinked, and a purple cloud formed between two trees, looking like a hammock from the stars. "Kill the man in the morning. Yes?"

Pirouz nodded his head. "Yes." Pirouz climbed into the hammock cloud and shut his eyes.

The next morning, it felt like the inferno Pirouz had seen the previous evening was an ocean away. Once Pirouz opened his eyes and got up, taking in the bright morning sun shining down on the green field and apple trees, he thought of the mountain of bones and the brutality of the man killing the other. He thought of the dragon, knowing that it was no hallucination. His stomach felt awful, like it was full of air. It was the kind of feeling one wakes up to when they know there is a task to be performed. In this case, it was murder. But still, he thought, staring straight up at the apples hanging from the tree branches above his head. *That beast was summoned by the Shaman and that beast has caused an odd chaos, so shouldn't the Shaman be stopped? After all, for someone to have the power to summon such a thing, shouldn't that be considered? Also: I NEED to find out who killed Míngzé.* Pirouz sat up on the purple hammock cloud, then stepped off of it. It vanished into the air. Pirouz looked at where it once was, then noticed a tray of breakfast placed on one of the boulders near one of the trees.

Pirouz ate the breakfast; it was eggs and cuts of lamb. There was also a jug of ice cold water, which Pirouz finished half of the jug. He stretched, meditated, then started to walk over to the grassy hill to kill the Shaman. A part of him wished he could just lie in the grass and enjoy the day, yet when he saw the stone hut, he knew it was too late. A man with wild hair was hanging up sheets. When he noticed Pirouz standing on top of the hill, he dropped a wet sheet on the ground.

"Conjurer of the Hell Dragon, I have come here to end your life. I have been sent by the Hell Dragon himself."

"Very well. If that is your intention..." The Shaman raised his hands, and he jabbed them forward, creating a brilliant pink and blue light around his fists that fired towards Pirouz. "...Die."

Chapter 9: Cult of Doom

The light blast zapped itself into the ground just as Pirouz barely dodged it with a quick leap to the nearest apple tree. He stood on the branch as the smoke blew in the wind and took out his sword. The Shaman zapped another light blast at Pirouz, demolishing the tree in an explosion of blue and pink sparks and smoke. Pirouz landed on the ground in his fighting stance. *His chi energy is so strong he is able to send power blasts that will surely kill me if I am not careful!* Another light blast was fired, this time hitting Pirouz's sword and forcing him off his feet, flying back, smashing into a tree so hard it snapped back. *I hate this guy,* Pirouz thought. He jumped to his feet and did the only thing he *could* do: he charged. As he ran, he jumped wildly to his left and right, dodging a series of light blasts that went off like deadly fireworks in the dirt, blowing craters into the ground.

The second Pirouz reached the Shaman, leaving a trail of smoked-out holes in the ground behind him, the Shaman raised his hand, and a saber flew towards him, fully unsheathed. Pirouz took notice of the Shaman's technique. He was using the nine swords of Dugu technique, one taught at The House of Poison. He thought, as they exchanged blow after blow, creating even more fireworks with the sparks between the blades, that despite the Shaman's mastery of chi, his sword technique was rigid. Pirouz could see it, as he had trained at The House of Poison, the greatest martial arts school in the known martial world. He did not train in just one technique... he trained in *all of them.*

If I can stay close to him, he will not use his chi energy blasts against me. Pirouz could sense the Shaman tiring out as Pirouz did his tornado attack, forcing the Shaman's back to the grey wall of the stone hut. The Shaman jerked his head to the side, causing Pirouz's sword to hit the wall. His blade absorbed the vibration. Pirouz stepped back, then continued his attack. He did a back flip, kicking the Shaman in the chin, causing him to fall flat on his back. Pirouz then stepped over the Shaman's body and stomped on his wrist, causing him to release his sword. Pirouz kicked the weapon away. He pointed the tip of his sword right under the Shaman's jugular, who seemed too exhausted to fight back.

Pirouz raised his sword, ready to hack the Shaman's throat open, when he heard a sound: A woman and a child, crying. Pirouz looked behind him. A woman who appeared to be about a decade younger than the Shaman, holding a little boy. Both were crying.

"Please don't kill my husband! I beg of you! We know he did wrong, summoning the dragon, but he is trying to make it right! Please! Look into the eyes of his son!" Pirouz took this sight in. He paused. All that could be heard was the Shaman panting, the woman and boy crying, the wind blowing through the trees, and many birds chirping.

Pirouz sheathed his sword. "I apologize." He bowed his head slightly. "Forgive me." His eyes went to the woman holding the child. He repeated, "Forgive me." Then turned his attention back to the Shaman. "The dragon sent me to kill you."

"I would have thought so," The Shaman said. He lowered his hands. "Otherwise, you would have had to be crazy or stupid, and you do not look crazy." He took a closer look at Pirouz. "You do not look from here. What brings you to the mountain, young man? You are quite skilled."

"I am here seeking vengeance."

"Yes... Aren't we all." He extended his hand. "I welcome you to tea."

The walls of the stone hut were an ocean blue color, and there was an elaborately decorated rug beneath Pirouz's feet. The little boy kept to himself, playing with a wooden sword outside while his parents served Pirouz the tea, asking him to sit down on the carpet in the middle of the room. The Shaman blew on the steaming beverage, sipped on it, then said: "The only reason you are alive is because I am most curious."

"This smells amazing," Pirouz said. "Thank you." He sipped on the tea. "Oh my, this is great stuff." He looked at the Shaman. "Oh yes, forgive me, yeah, ask me anything."

"Would you prefer to remain vague on your reasons for vengeance?"

"Yes. I hope you don't think that's rude, especially with you giving me this amazing tea."

"No, I do not. You are smart."

"Can *I* ask you a question?"

"Of course."

"Why'd you summon that thing?" Pirouz's face looked like a puzzled animal when he asked this.

"I needed the dragon to make a wish come true... that is usually why one would summon a lucky dragon."

"That's a *lucky* dragon?"

"That's only one half of it."

"What do you mean?"

"That dragon has another version of itself, one that is more... kind shall we say..."

"Oh?"

"Yes. You see... the reason the twin dragons are even on this island is because of me. Yes, I admit it. But I had a partner in all of this. This was just three summers ago. My son, the one playing outside without a care in the world, was dying of an unknown disease. His skin had become almost green, his breathing was labored and heavy, and he was often coughing a horrid amount of mucus. You are young, chances are you do not yet know the pain of being a parent and seeing your child be at the mercy of the cruelty of nature." The Shaman looked at his wife, then back at Pirouz. "Can you imagine being a mother and nurturing this human being, only to see him... succumb to disease?"

"I cannot," Pirouz said. "I cannot imagine that pain, I am sorry."

"Don't be." The Shaman laughed. "I don't want to say

things worked out in the end, but my son is alive, so that is good." His face turned serious. "I knew a man- not very well- but I met him when I was a street performer. He was a master of the martial arts, though he remained mysterious about where he was schooled and who he had worked for." He downed half of his tea. "This man... he had an odd thing... with power. He seemed to crave it to such a degree that he was willing to fool everyone about his true nature. He presented himself like a noble practitioner of the martial arts, but I always suspected he had underworld ties- if not the House of Poison or one of the wolf clans or any number of bandit groups."

Pirouz was listening intently; he felt as though something important was coming to light, something that had to do directly with him and his mission on the mountain. "What was his interest in *you*?"

The Shaman continued: "I am a shaman, boy. A shaman, when properly in tune with the universe, can bring forth many great things... but that is not what we are for. We are not to be exploited, but used as guides. At the time, what I wanted to learn from him was the way of the martial arts, which he seemed to know instinctively, like breathing. He would disappear for long periods, but he would always come back with more lessons that I learned to combine with my own mastery of chi energy."

Hence the star fire power, thought Pirouz.

"From the time that I knew him, he was obsessed with the legend of the two-sided dragon."

"The two-sided dragon is the one that sent me to kill you?"

"Yes, he is one half of it."

"Where is the other half?"

"The other half is being held prisoner... by the man I speak of. You see, to summon the dragon, a scroll had to be read aloud by someone who could act as a gateway between our world and the spirit realm, which is what a shaman does. The scroll was guarded by a warrior who was entrusted to guard it with his life, and so, I used him to kill the guard of the scroll, and he used me to recite its passage, and that was when the two-sided dragon came to our world, banished to the mountain."

"So where is the other one?"

"The Knuckles crew is holding him."

"The Knuckles crew? Are those the idiots who followed the Skull Crusher? Skull Crusher is dead; they should scatter like the idiots they are."

"They followed the Skull Crusher, who followed the hell dragon. The fact that Skull Crusher is dead is irrelevant to them."

"What happened to the man, the master of martial arts?"

"When the dragon was summoned, he learned a spell to enslave one of them, and so he holds onto it, in the strongest of chains that were forged in the darkest of magic, trying to figure out how to harness its powers."

"Did this man have a name?"

"He always had me refer to him as Purple Lizard. Since the end of our partnership, I know now the significance of that name: Purple, because purple is the most opulent of colors, and this man adored opulence, and lizard, because like a lizard, he was sneaky."

Pirouz needed to enquire further: "What were his martial arts skills like?"

"He was the greatest martial artist I had ever seen. Funny enough, you somewhat remind me of him; you have similar styles.

Could this man have been in the House of Poison? Pirouz wondered. "What did he look like?"

"He was a rugged fellow, that's all I remember. He shaved his face; however, he never liked to look unkempt. He just had a face that had seen much violence. He was tall as well."

"Did this man wear a mask?"

"Yes, he enjoyed wearing masks. His favorite mask was the one he wore all the time... that of a man who was whatever you needed him to be... so long as you allowed him to take advantage."

"The vengeance I am seeking on this island is against a

man in a mask," Pirouz said.

"Yes, that makes sense. Describe the mask, if you will." Pirouz described the mask. The Shaman simply nodded his head in recognition. "Yes, that is Purple Lizard."

"Tell me where he is... and I will kill him."

"Even with him surrounded by the Knuckle Army."

"I don't care," Pirouz said, getting up. "I will go in there, in disguise... and I will assassinate him."

"In disguise? You know how the Knuckle Army dresses?"

"I wasted a few of them before I met the dragon. They were covered from head to toe."

"That is pretty close to suicide."

"That has been a theme of my trip."

"I will accompany you." The Shaman stood up. "The only reason I did not go before, to the knuckle army camp, is because I was but one man."

"Darling, don't go!" The Shaman's wife shouted. The Shaman held her gently by the shoulders. "My love, I must..." The Shaman looked at Pirouz. "Would you excuse us for a moment?" Pirouz nodded his head, downed the last of his tea, and got up and left. Before he was out into the open air, the Shaman said, without turning around: "Wait for me. I won't be long." Pirouz went outside and could hear the Shaman and his wife arguing. To stop hearing what they were saying, he busied himself by climbing up one of the apple trees and grabbing himself one.

"Have you ever had a black diamond apple?" The little boy asked.

Pirouz looked at him while on the branch. "No, I haven't, but I've heard of them!"

"There's a tree of them over there!" The boy pointed his chubby finger at a tree just a short distance away from the one Pirouz was hanging on.

"Oh, that's neat!" Pirouz jumped off the tree branch and went over to the black diamond tree. He had heard of the trees from Master Yuze, who said that there were rare apple trees that produced apples that were as black as night. Pirouz looked at the apples, which looked like ink spots dotting a tree, with wonder.

"Try one!" The boy shouted.

"No, I think these are rare; your father probably wouldn't like me having one. I think I'll have one of the other ones."

"Try one, I insist." The voice of the Shaman creaked out from behind Pirouz, who turned around.

"Are you sure? Black diamond apples are legendary and rare."

"Yes, I know. It's okay. At the end of the day, black or red, an apple is an apple. Let's go." Pirouz followed the Shaman, who walked briskly. After a few steps through the tall grass, the Shaman held out his hand and opened it. He held a glass ball full of some sort of purple liquid. "Do you see this?"

"Yeah. What is it?"

"It's a little ball full of a liquid I made that explodes when you throw it. I am going to use these to level the Knuckle Army and kill Purple Lizard."

Pirouz had seen various exploding weapons from his days being raised by The House of Poison. There was something that felt strange to him about it, a weapon that can kill just by being thrown or dropped or hit. He did not think it wrong or right, just strange. "Can I see one of them explode?" Pirouz asked.

"And waste them? Absolutely not."

"How many do you have?"

"I have a bunch."

"Then show me. I want to know what we're working with, here. I can help you strategize."

"You're just a boy who wants to see something explode."

"Yes, I admit to that. Please, sir, oh great shaman, show me."

"Very well. We could go for some fish. We'll stop at my fishing hole just a little way away, and we can throw one in the lake."

"Does it kill the fish?"

"Yes, that's why I invented it. I call them star balls."

"Wow, what a stupid thing to call them, no offense."

The Shaman scowled: "It's easy for a young person to sit back and critique the accomplishments of their elders."

"I'm sorry, that was wrong. Is that your fishing spot?" Pirouz pointed to a glistening blue lake shimmering in the distance.

"Yes, that's the one." Once they reached the fishing hole, Pirouz took in the sight of fish, countless fish of all sorts of colors and shapes. "So, what you want to do is crush it in your hand, then throw it." He tossed one to Pirouz.

Pirouz almost dropped it, startled. "Whoa, it won't explode if you just throw it?"

"No," the Shaman said. "Examine it."

Pirouz held the ball up; it seemed to be made of a glass-like substance that was clear, like a hardened gel. Inside, the purple substance was separated by a wall. On one side, there was a dark purple gel, spotted with bubbles that didn't move. On the other side, a lighter shade of purple with the same amount of motionless bubbles. "There are two special gels I created in there. Alone, they are harmless. When combined, however, they become combustible. Watch." The Shaman held up one of the shiny purple balls, squeezed it, then threw it into the fishing hole as hard as he could. Not a moment later, the water exploded in a furious blast that sent it all up into the air, then come raining down on the two along with a scattered array of fish, flapping on the grass.

"That was really neat," Pirouz said, watching the remaining water in the fishing hole wave back and forth, recovering from the blast. "Can I try?"

"Yes, but don't blast the water, throw it at that little tree over there."

Pirouz, with glee, made sure the Shaman was well out of the way, then threw one of the exploding balls at the tiny waist-high tree the Shaman pointed out. The tree vanished in a flash, leaving a hole in the ground. Pirouz said, tactfully, after calming down from the explosion, "I would ask for another, yet I know we must conserve them." He then asked: "What do you call these things again?"

"Star balls."

Pirouz and the Shaman set out for the Knuckle Army camp, on the other side of the mountain. "You must have been startled to see all those dead bodies with the dragon," the Shaman said.

"I *did* wonder how they all got there."

"There is a large, somewhat peaceful village at the bottom of the other side of the mountain. You never hear about them because there is nothing violent about them. The most interesting thing about them is they are a pearl-diving village, at least a good portion of them are... or were."

"So all those bones are from that village?"

"Mostly. Those people were not martial artists; they were peace-loving people. When the dragon came, he infected their minds with promises of riches, and so they all went up to the mountain, and they all died."

"*All* of them?"

"Well, no. A few remained." He shook his head. "A lot of widows. It's very sad."

"That dragon really shook things up, didn't he?"

"Yes, I feel bad."

"At least you feel bad."

The Shaman stopped. "You hear that?"

Pirouz stopped and put his hand up, trying to listen. He could hear the grunting sound of men training, possibly doing punches in the air, followed by a shout.

"The Knuckles Army camp is close by."

"So what do we do?"

"I thought you would know."

"Sir." Pirouz gave the Shaman a *Really?* Look. "It was clear you were sort of leading this thing. I didn't even know this island had a damn dragon before literally last night." The Shaman simply shrugged. "Alright, follow me." Pirouz leapt up into the tree, jumping from branch to branch until he was at the top. The trees were too thick to see anything, but the sound became even clearer. He motioned for the Shaman to follow him. They leapt across a dozen trees, then stopped. "They are very close," Pirouz whispered. He smelled the air; it smelled of urine. He could see some empty cups placed at the trunk of the tree they were on top of. "Some of them come here to piss."

"Hopefully two come to piss at the same time."

"I don't think that will happen, but hey, we can hope."

They waited. After a while, they could not help but pass the time by whispering to one another. "Purple Lizard always seemed like he belonged to something... bigger."

"You think it's this? The Knuckle Army?" Pirouz asked.

"No. The Knuckle Army has only been around as long as the dragon. I told you earlier, I am fairly certain he was with the House of Poison."

"What makes you say that?"

"Have you *heard* of the House of Poison?"

"No, I can't say that I have."

"Some people don't even believe in them; they think they are a legend."

"What are they, then?"

"They started out as a group of martial artists who also made various poisons. I hear they help pull the strings of the world. They are like the Crimson Wolves, only secret. Really, though, I think they're just greedy thugs when you think about it. All they do is control things and murder people?"

"They murder people?"

"They work with the government, of course they murder people."

"Wow. That's interesting." Pirouz took a second to ponder this. He never thought of the group to which he belonged as a gang of thugs, and he thought about the implications of that. "Well I don't know anything about the House of Poison. As I said earlier, I am just a young adventurer, but that is some really interesting stuff. *Very* interesting. Secret societies and whatnot."

"Sssshh," the Shaman said as the sound of feet stepping

on leaves cracked through the forest. A member of the Knuckle Army was making his way just under the tree to urinate. He was about to go about his business; that was when Pirouz leapt down from the tree and knocked him out cold with a clean kick to the head. He was undoing his armor when the Shaman jumped down to the forest ground, right in front of Pirouz. "What are you doing?"

"I'm getting into the Knuckle uniform."

"No, no, I want to."

"Why?" Pirouz was a little exasperated to hear this.

"Because I think it will work best that way. On second thought, we should have discussed this."

"Do you want to wait for another guy to come take a piss?"

"That would be preferable. What was your plan?"

"I was going to put these clothes on, and you would wait back here and do your fireworks thing if I get caught."

"That's your plan?"

"Yeah, I was going to free the dragon, see what happens - you wait here, what's the big deal?"

"I'm not waiting here."

"Neither am I!"

More footsteps on dead leaves could be heard. Pirouz leapt back up into the tree, carrying the unconscious body of the Knuckle soldier with him. The Shaman looked alarmed, then followed, flying straight up into the tree.

"Our leader will be speaking soon. Get all your piss out of the way, because last time he killed a man who went to relieve himself during his speech." Two soldiers were now under the tree, preparing to urinate. Pirouz wasted no time; he jumped back down to the forest floor and sent eight rhythmic punches to each face, knocking both men out.

Pirouz looked up. He did a whisper shout: "Come on! Your prayers have been answered!" The Shaman jumped back down. They began unfastening the belts around the Knuckle Army uniforms when they heard another set of footsteps. "Damnit!" Pirouz said. He then jumped back up into the tree, this time carrying both men with him. The Shaman jumped up as well. They saw a young foot soldier get into the urination area, go about his business, then leave. Pirouz and the Shaman decided to change in the tree, which was difficult but doable. The two were now fully clothed in the Knuckles Army uniform. They leapt down and looked up at the soldier up in the trees. "It'll be a while before they come to. Come on, be cool."

Pirouz and the Shaman, with their faces concealed under the masks of the uniform, did their best to look casual and calm as they walked out onto the Knuckles Army camp. Pirouz could not help but remember his recent experience with Xi and the Crimson Wolf Clan. For some reason, he knew that this would not resolve itself as peacefully as what went down before.

"Brothers! The master is almost going to speak! This is your final warning! Get into positions!" Pirouz noticed the man shouting this from a stage. He looked indistinguishable from the rest of the soldiers. Pirouz looked at the Shaman, asking silently with his eyes, *What do you think "position" is?* The Shaman simply shrugged without shrugging, conveying the shrug with his eyes, silently, like Pirouz. Pirouz simply moved as all the other men did; the camp was now men, shoulder to shoulder, standing in a pit before the speech.

A voice grumbled—a voice that was deep yet still managed to overpower the sound of the entire murmuring camp: "We own the power to incinerate worlds." The entire camp fell silent. "The power to bring down kingdoms and make the entire world fall before us... but therein lies our responsibility." Pirouz noticed the words were coming from a man on stage. His back was to everyone. He certainly had to be the Purple Lizard, as his uniform was in the most opulent shades of purple. "A responsibility, entrusted to me..." His head arched down, and his arms extended. "To lead... to the best of my abilities." His hands fell to his side. "Some days... I do not want to lead. Some days I would like to be just a common man, like you all once more, before your purpose revealed itself to you. To live the life of a simple man who knows nothing of the machinations of the world and the cosmos. Can you imagine how peaceful that would be, my children? To have a family to look after, and to have a simple job in life, like a fisherman or one who hunts." He stepped out and faced the crowd. He was wearing the same mask as Míngzé's killer, and Pirouz could sense that it was the same man he had seen back at Auntie's inn.

The man in the mask, who Pirouz was now calling Purple Lizard in his head, walked up to a massive piece of fabric that was flowing in the wind, right in front of him at the back of the stage. He yanked it. The fabric flowed off to the ground, showing that underneath it was a dragon, the same size and shape as the Hell Dragon, only colorful and pretty, though weak-looking. The scales looked like individual gemstones that changed color slightly as the beast breathed in and out. The chains around it looked like they were made from glowing blue glass, though it was quite clear that it was some sort of metal forged in magic. The eyes of the dragon were barely open, and it looked like it had been drugged. Pirouz thought to himself about the lessons in the various poisons the house worked with. There was one poison that was never used. It was a sticky green substance that made liquid strings when you took a needle and poked it. He remembered this substance quite well. He thought of the day he first saw such a poison.

Several summers ago...
Cong, Yuze, Jiao Long, Míngzé, and Zhang Li were taking inventory of their poisons. Naturally, they were arguing. Zhang Li was chastising the men as Pirouz tried to stay out of the way, sweeping the floor. "You guys seem not to put these jars back in order on purpose." She said, placing a vial of *Bloody Eyes,* a homemade poison Zhang Li herself created, on the cupboard. She then went over to the box where a scorpion, centipede, and snake were fighting to the death. She caught the fight just as the snake, battle-scarred and bleeding from the scorpion, devoured the centipede. "Pirouz, look," said Zhang Li. Pirouz put the broom down and looked into

the cage. The scorpion popped its stinger into the snake's eye, paralyzing its head- killing it. "This will create something truly deadly," she said. Young Pirouz thought about how, through that murderous scene, a poison would be created that would influence the world in one way or another: through death. "Thank you for sweeping, Pirouz. If it weren't for you, this place would be a mess."

"You can say what you want to say, Zhang Li," Yuze said. "There's no need to be subtle with your brothers."

"Brother, Zhang Li is right, we cannot let our home become a mess. It will be our undoing." Cong said, straightening the jars of the various poisons.

"Young Pirouz is smart because he listens to a smart lady." Jiao Long was smiling as he said this.

"Don't try to flatter me. I know your tricks, Jiao Long." Zhang Li said, shaking her head while she wiped the dust off of a jar.

"Pirouz, come, look at this." Míngzé said. Pirouz went from the little box of venomous animal death to where Míngzé was sitting, staring at a large jar that was full of what looked like a green syrup that had a slight glow to it. "Have you ever wondered how to poison a dragon?"

"I have actually," Pirouz said, because he, in fact, had.

"This is how. This is the only known dragon poison in the world."

"Have you ever used it?" Pirouz asked.

"Once." Master Míngzé said. He smiled. "It was a horrible story." He grabbed a large needle that was as long as his forearm and dipped it into the jar, pulling out a dab of it left a trail of gel string in the air. "This much will make a dragon go sleepy sleepy."

"Try not to break the bottle, Míngzé." Yuze said. "You never know when a dragon may show up."

Pirouz thought of that day as the man in the mask spoke further, in front of the crowd of the Knuckle Army, standing before a large and beautiful drugged dragon. "This is how the world will fall and pray to us. For we must lead. The people do not know that they need our guidance, but when they receive it, they will see that they can never do without it." He took a few steps up stage and put up his hands. "My humble soldiers, I ask that today you think of the new world as you go about the day. Think of the fact that you are playing an instrumental part in it happening. The world will go from chaos to structure, because it must. In order to do that, we must go to the Shaman and demand that he cast the spell to release the dragons from the island so we can conquer the world. We have been looking for this bastard for quite some time. Now, we have found him. One of our foot soldiers happened upon a hut where he saw the Shaman's wife and son. He hurried back to tell us. We are going back this evening to retrieve them. Soon we can ride both dragons to the rest of the world. With the spells that the Shaman knows, there will be no end to how we can utilize these beasts for our own purposes! That is why he hides, like a coward! I mentioned the simple life, the life of a simple man who does simple things. Do you know what my opinion is of that, ultimately? It is weak; that is why the Shaman retreated to have a family, because he was weak. He could not take the task of leading the world, but I can. Let us lead! Let us lead! Let us lead!" This began a chant. As the men chanted, Pirouz did not think anyone would notice if he said to the Shaman:

"They are going to kill your wife and kid!"

"Not if I kill them first!" The Shaman looked like he was ready to start hacking away at the soldiers, but Pirouz stopped him by grabbing his shoulder.

"We have to beat them to it!"

The Shaman snarled, "I'll kill them all for even thinking of it!" The Shaman raised his fist, gripping the glass ball full of the two purple liquids, then threw it up into the air and ran. Pirouz ran as well, in the opposite direction. The star ball spun in the air, stopping for a moment, high above the Knuckle Army, then fell, hit the ground, and burst. The blast was strong enough to push Pirouz to the ground, skidding in the dirt belly-first, while Knuckle Army soldiers flew in every direction, mangled and confused from the blast. Pirouz could feel his ears ringing. He turned on his back and looked up at the sky. For a moment, all looked peaceful, for he could only see the clouds and the blue sky above. Then he noticed two men fly directly over him, like they were being thrown by someone- that someone being the Shaman. Pirouz jumped up to his feet. Dust was making it nearly impossible to see; he could only see the chaos of Knuckle Army soldiers running in every direction. Beyond that, the stage seemed to disappear in the dust. Pirouz tried to find a way out of the dust cloud, noticing that no one was noticing him. The cloud started to clear, and the stage could be seen once again, with the giant dragon still lying there. The Purple Lizard, however, was nowhere to be seen.

"He was with that one!" Pirouz heard a voice shout amidst the chaos. He turned around and noticed a keen-eyed Knuckle Army soldier pointing at him and shouting the words at the top of his lungs. "Kill the intruder!" A long line of Knuckle Army soldiers in front of Pirouz turned to face who was being pointed at. They all attacked at once. Not a moment too soon, Pirouz's sword was out and slicing away, causing mists and geysers of blood to gush from each soldier's wound. A larger-than-average soldier rumbled toward Pirouz, holding two mallets. Pirouz dodged a blow, then stuck his sword into the soldier's gut and ripped it out, causing blood and intestines to spill and slop onto the newly minted battlefield.

An explosion blasted Pirouz across the battlefield, sending a sting through his left hand. Landing on the other side, Pirouz sat, about to stand when he saw the stage zap into a flash of smoke and fire. The chains surrounding the dragon turned red-hot, then melted into lava, streaming down the scaly body of the dragon. The Shaman leapt up into the trees, tossing one of the explosion orbs behind him, flinging ten knuckle soldiers across the sky. *He ditched me,* Pirouz thought. Right at that moment, he felt a shadow extend over him as he lay on his back. His eyes took a moment to adjust, and he could see it was Purple Lizard. Purple Lizard reached down and picked Pirouz up by the throat, holding him in the air. He ripped Pirouz's mask off. "Pirouz, your other masters will be most disappointed." He brought Pirouz, whose legs were dangling in the air, closer to him. "When they see that you are dead."

It was at that moment Pirouz knew who Purple Lizard was, from the growl in his voice, to the look in his eyes. He could see the essence of Purple Lizard with him holding his throat with the threat of breaking his neck like it were a twig, for he had felt those hands before in combat. He ripped the mask off with his free hand to confirm. He was right.

It was master Yuze.

Chapter 10:
A Proper Goodbye

The oxygen was cut from Pirouz's windpipe by the way Master Yuze was holding him, causing Pirouz to pass out.

He awoke in the dungeon. At first, he thought he had died and gone to some sort of underworld. The second he started to feel the pain of the cold steel cuffs digging into his skin, he knew he was quite alive. He waited, for what felt like days, with rats that went in and out of the room through the barred door, the only thing that kept him company. Finally, the door opened. A shadow stood in front of the light. Pirouz squinted; he could barely see. "Hello, my student." Master Yuze stepped out of the shadows. "Here we are."

"Why?" was all Pirouz could mutter.

"Pirouz, you're young. It's difficult to grasp the... complicated nature of the world."

"You killed Master Míngzé?!"

"Yes, I did." He stepped deeper into the cell, then slammed the door behind him.

"Why? He was your sworn brother."

"Again, Pirouz... the world is a complicated place." He smiled. "It's a fun fantasy... a world where all men act honorably... but it's not so, young one."

"Are you denying you have *any*? Our way of life is founded on it- that's what *you* taught me!"

"I was playing a part, young prince. You may have perceived Míngzé and me to be brothers... but the truth is we had a difference of opinion in terms of the direction of The House of Poison." He looked outside, examining the stars. "He wanted us to concentrate on medicines. He said our knowledge of what different substances do to one's body was put to waste... on killing." He looked at Pirouz. "Can you imagine wanting to throw away what we have built? For the *illusion* of helping people?"

"Míngzé was a good man, he could have helped people if he wanted to... and he was still alive."

"Míngzé was just a killer who wanted to clean his conscience." He grumbled a deep laugh. "I saw that man kill many... *many* human beings. He could see the end of his life and he thought he could somehow... change things. But I knew..." Yuze stepped over to Pirouz: "Once a killer, always a killer." His smile turned into a frightening scowl. "Where's the Shaman and his family."

"How am I supposed to know? I'm here. Last I saw, he blew the chains off that dragon."

"You must have had a plan going in. In case things didn't go your way."

"The whole reason I'm even *here* is because we barely had a plan."

"WHERE'S MY DRAGON?" His voice was now in a rage.

"HE'S ON THE DAMN MOON!! I DON'T KNOW!"

Yuze brought out a sword, from the shine and shape, from its sheer beauty, Pirouz knew right away that it was the Savior Sword. "Much blood was spilled to forge this steel. Many, many men were stabbed or beaten bloody, then all of their blood was drained just for a tiny bit of iron so this magnificent weapon could be forged. This is what you're here for, aren't you? You have this fantasy of taking this beautiful weapon from the island and showing it to your other masters so they can give you a nice pat on the head, and you can finally feel accepted... The truth is... you never will. You will never... ever... feel welcomed anywhere, because you're just the bastard prince." He brought the tip of the blade up to Pirouz's chin and pressed it lightly, causing a bead of blood to form and slide down the iron. "You want to know something funny?" There was a pause. "Míngzé and I are the ones who killed that little girlfriend of your's parents. Isn't that funny? She thinks the Crimson Wolf Clan was behind it- and they were -but *we* were the ones who led the charge."

Pirouz felt his stomach drop. "That's not true, you're just

trying to mess with my mind. It's not working."

"Believe me, prince bastard, if I wanted to mess with your mind, your head would come off..." He stepped back, leaning against the stone wall. "We. Killed. Her parents... and you want to know the best part? Now she knows. She's been briefed on it, my little spies in that little gang have told me."

"I hate you, Yuze. I want you to know that."

"Good... you're not so simple after all. You have enough common sense to hate." He looked back out the window. "We are going to torture you until you tell us anything you may have been withholding about the Shaman. I want my dragon back... I am going to *get* my dragon back... then... I am going to fly off of this island, and I am going to kill the other members of the House of Poison, and I will start anew." A man entered the room, he was wearing a cloak and looked at Pirouz with a smile. One of his eyes bulged oddly. "This is my number one torturer. You two are going to get to know each other quite well. Have you ever wanted to torture royal blood?"

"Yes sir... yes sir I have."

"Well, now's your chance." Yuze looked at Pirouz. "I'm not going to say sorry, boy... but there is a part of me that wishes you had stayed in the land where your father's blood was spilled. Have a good night." Yuze walked out of the dungeon, slamming the door behind him. He shouted: "You have a key, right?"

"Yes sir, yes sir I do."

"Wonderful, have fun doing your thing."

"Thank you sir. I will have fun doing my thing, I will." The torturer sat down in front of Pirouz with a smile, like a child being told a story. "They beat you quite badly, but there was no point to it, as you were barely conscious after the first man hit you on the head. Not our master, but the men who took to your body when our master threw you to them. Would you like to see some wonderful things?" He got back up, went to the door, stuck a lock in the keyhole, opened it, then pulled in a leather sack that seemed full of metal objects with the way it clinked and clanked. He got up and sat down again, this time sliding the leather bag in front of him. "The first tool is basic." He pulled out two blades held together with a nail. "I'm going to use this to cut off your little bits first. By little bits I mean your little bits, your fingers, your toes, anything that goes wiggle wiggle." Pirouz said nothing. The torturer continued: "This right here I like to use..." He pulled out a curved blade about the size of a large leg bone, "To skin." He smiled. "You may ask yourself how much I skin. Well, if I have the person for a long time, I can stretch out the skinning to last months, years if I wanted to. It would be something that my pets start to look forward to because it's a break from the bone-pulverizing methods. Look." He pulled out a mallet and a chisel. "Common workman tools are the best for these things."

"So, you're a craftsman, basically." He was genuinely interested, despite the horror to come.

"Yes, yes, yes! A craftsman! A craftsman of pain and suffering! Do you know what a subtle cruelty I enjoy here?"

"No, please tell me."

"We made this dungeon from a hole in a big rock on the side of the mountain. I asked the master Purple Lizard if we could have windows in some of the cells. Do you know why?"

"Why?"

"Because to have the outside world just out of your reach... that is a wonderful torture. To see the stars and the moon, to hear crickets outside... and to know you can never experience those things freely or without pain, that is a wonderful torture! A wonderful torture indeed!"

"You certainly have an interesting view on how to have a good time."

The torturer waddled toward Pirouz and punched him in the face, hard. "That'll teach you to get too cute with me. In the world of pain you're about to enter, that was a friendly pat on the back. I'll be back to cut off your bits." The torturer left the cell, slamming the door shut so hard Pirouz could feel the rock shake.

The sounds of crickets and a stream of water trickling somewhere were all Pirouz could hear. It was then that, feeling hopeless, Pirouz cried. *Please, if anyone can hear me… please help me. I hate this place.* He both thought these words and said them lightly. He slumped his head forward and grunted, suppressing his tears. *Master Míngzé would not approve of me crying,* he thought. He rubbed his fingers into the palm of his hand and felt dry blood and a dull pain from an sharp object buried in his flesh. He could feel what it was: A metal splinter. It must have been from the Shaman's explosions. He felt the length of his palm and realized the splinter was quite large. It had somehow buried itself in Pirouz's palm during the blast, and he was in such a daze that he didn't register it. He wedged his fingers into the wound and slid out the pick-like metal piece. He then jammed the pick into the keyhole of his chains. After jiggling it around for no longer than a few moments, the chains opened, releasing him to the ground.

Pirouz hit the ground and grunted. *Thank you.* He thought to himself. He clenched his fists and pounded them against the ground just once, then got up. He looked out the window, noticing, in the sky, the awesome sight of the dragon, floating amongst the stars. The dragon looked bigger and it looked as though the red dragon and the one in chains had combined. Pirouz's stomach dropped at the sight of the thing. It looked magnificent. It was on a side of the mountain where no one could see but Pirouz.

"Young Prince…" The dragon said, his voice echoing through the air. For some reason, Pirouz could sense that only he could hear the dragon, as though it was communicating with his mind. "You made me whole… I am both the red dragon and the dragon of light… I was split in two by the Purple Lizard's spells… now I am free. I would like to give you a gift. Step to the side, please." Pirouz did what the dragon said. The moment he did so, a blast of fire came into the cell straight from the dragon's mouth. The fire shot directly at the chains that were holding Pirouz. The chains turned bright red, glowing, then they melted into the shape of a full suit of armor, a sword, and a shield. The orange glow cooled down, then settled into a metallic red color. The helmet of armor was in the shape of a lion. Smoke smoldered off the surface of the metal, then vanished, leaving a flawless metal armor that had a rouge shine. The scarf with the crystal sparrow drifted into the cell from outside, as though it fell from the sky.

Pirouz had the armor on with the scarf safely nestled inside. It all fit perfectly. He looked at the helmet and the sword, which were sitting there on the stone floor of the dungeon cell. He first picked the helmet up and slipped it on. A surge spread through his body, an energy he could not begin to describe. He then picked up the sword. The muscles in his arm pumped as he held up the weapon. A light blasted from his arm to the blade, flashing out at the tip. He did not want to wait; thus, he was happy when he heard the dungeon door open. It creaked forward, he could hear the unsettling giggles of the torturer on the other side.

"We shall begin!" he said with glee from behind the open door. He poked his head in to look inside. His bag dropped as the door fully opened, revealing Pirouz in the red, shining lion armor. Pirouz held his sword up. "GUARDS! GUARDS! GUA-" Pirouz sliced the top half of the torturer's head, it spun in the air like a top and plopped onto the ground, making a cracking sound. It looked like a hairy bowl full of brain soup. Pirouz looked from the head top on the floor back to the door, where the torturer slumped forward in a spray of blood. Four Knuckle Army guards burst forward with spears up.

"Come get some," Pirouz said. The guards rammed forward, spears up, but they were no match for the power and speed of Pirouz's moves. It seemed as though the armor tapped into a hidden power. His sword left a blue electric trail, and the blade left a hazy road of blood in the air as it cut through each member of the Knuckle Army that burst through the door. Pirouz reduced the first four Knuckle Army soldiers to crying men with bloody stumps- one split in half from the waist. Pirouz stepped through the bodies and out of the cell. The dungeon hall was cavernous with torches lighting the way. He could see what was clearly the exit in the form of a blue stone door. He confidently strode down the hall where more

Knuckle Army soldiers attacked and were reduced to bloody stumps and bodies. The number of soldiers rushing out to kill was so high, and Pirouz's attacks so ferocious, it was like he was walking through a rainstorm of blood. Pirouz made it to the end of the hall and opened the stone door.

On the other side of the stone door, to Pirouz's surprise, was a garden with a walkway that was green with moss. Pirouz slammed the stone door shut behind him. Two Knuckle Army soldiers, clearly not knowing what was going on inside, were asleep on a stone bench. "I just killed and maimed a bunch of your comrades," Pirouz said. The two soldiers were startled awake.

"Eh?" One of them said, looking up at the rather frightening red metal lion in front of him. The other soldier raised his sword to strike, but his fingers, two of them, were sliced off while they were still gripping the blade. "I meant to cut off only two fingers. Imagine what it would be like if I wanted to cut out your heart." While the soldier with two missing fingers gasped and struggled to gather his two severed fingers from the ground, the other dropped his saber and made a salute to Pirouz. "Smart." Pirouz looked up. *So here I am,* he thought to himself. Just beyond a modest grassy hill above the garden was the temple, the very temple where the Savior Sword was rumored to be. "That is *the* temple, no?"

"Yes!" The Knuckle Army soldier shouted this, then bowed. Pirouz walked both soldiers to the rock door of the dungeon and had them get in. He then shut the door, instructing them to come out in a day, and only with the certainty that they would not try to retaliate. Pirouz then walked through the garden to the stone steps leading up to the grassy hill. There was a slight breeze, making the grass wave back and forth.

"Where did you get the lovely get-up, boy?" Master Yuze was silently watching Pirouz approach from beyond the steps of the temple.

"I am no boy, Purple Lizard. I am Pirouz, Prince of Persia and member of The House of Poison."

"Heh." Yuze snorted. "Why call me Purple Lizard now? I

prefer Yuze." Yuze took the Savior Sword out. It sparkled in the sunlight much like Pirouz's armor.

"I have no wish to banter with you... My only wish..." Pirouz got into his fighting stance, sword out. "Is for you to die."

"You first." Yuze said. He did a front flip towards Pirouz and struck at him in a lightning-like flash of steel, pounding at Pirouz's sword. The spark from the attack whizzed off the metal, lighting one of the surrounding trees on fire. The fire grew as the two fought. Yuze spun around and performed a smooth tornado attack, which Pirouz kept up with, causing a fireworks-like array of light between the clashing metals. Yuze managed to land a blow right at Pirouz's helmet, clanging it off and twirling it into the air, landing on the burning tree. He slashed toward Pirouz once more, slicing through his cheek. The blood poured down Pirouz's face. Pirouz backed away, gliding in the air using his lightness kung fu, landing on the steps of the temple.

"YOU ARE A LOWLY TRAITOR, YUZE! KNOW THAT, EVEN IF YOU KILL ME."

"I'm a member of the House of Poison, dumb prince... we are killers, not charity workers... your dead master's biggest mistake... was thinking killers like us..." He approached the steps. "Can be good." Yuze pumped the Savior Sword in the air. A green electric light blasted down from the blue clouds forming in the sky. Pirouz could see Yuze chanting to himself as the electric green coursed through the sword and his body. His eyes suddenly went green, an unnatural, glowing green that sparkled with similar-hued sparks. He growled ferociously and charged up the steps. The two clashed their swords against one another, only this time it was Pirouz on the defensive. Yuze was now past the steps on the marble floor of the main entrance of the temple. The two bashed their respective weapons against one another over and over while the trees just beyond the temple burned, causing embers and ash to float in the breeze like fireflies.

Yuze took a firm swing at Pirouz's eyes, but was blocked by Pirouz's shield. Pirouz landed a blow by bashing it against

Yuze's face, cracking his cheekbone. Pirouz swiped the shield against Yuze's face once more, then again and again, until Yuze was on the ground, his face a bloody pulp. Pirouz threw the shield to his side, spinning it in the air and causing it to slam into one of the burning trees. He then raised his sword above his head with both hands and slammed it down, directly into Yuze's bloody face. Blood gushed forth while another spray of red shot out the back of Yuze's skull. Pirouz could feel the tip of his sword scrape against the marble floor of the temple.

He plucked the sword out of his former master's head and held it up, then collapsed to his knees, exhausted. It began to rain, killing the fire that had lit the trees, causing them to mist with smoke. Pirouz looked at the Savior Sword, resting in Yuze's clenched fist. He pried it out of his dead fingers and looked at it. There was a design of a wolf's head at the base. It was a magnificent sword, and Pirouz had seen many. *My shifus back at the House of Poison will be most pleased*, Pirouz thought. He then went into the temple to shelter himself from the rain. After lying back on a marble bench near a shrine, he could hear an army of footsteps and chatter. Pirouz got up to see Xi, standing with Jia, at the entrance of the temple. The Crimson Wolf clan, an army of them, stood behind them.

"Jia, leave, wait outside with the others," Xi said, Pirouz got up from the bench as Jia obeyed Xi's command. Xi leaned toward Pirouz; her head tilted forward. He could not see her eyes well beyond the mask she wore. It was the same mask that allowed her to command an army. She screamed as she ran, fists up, and then grunted as she did her best to land a blow to Pirouz's face. He dodged each swipe, calmly, enraging her even further.

"YOU KILLED MY FAMILY!"

"I didn't."

"YOUR MASTER DID, YOU BASTARD!"

"The master that did is dead, Xi, and I did not."

"I won't rest until the House of Poison falls!"

"Okay then," Pirouz said with a calm regret in his voice. Xi stopped punching and kicking at Pirouz.

Her lip trembled with emotion when she said, "I thought you were my friend."

"I am your friend." Pirouz said. "And I only found out what happened after we departed... It's the way of my world." Xi buried her head in her hands and cried. Pirouz could sense that in her heart, she knew he was telling the truth. Pirouz looked down at the marble floor, then to Xi, the sight of her crying shattered him inside, and all he could say- the only thing that made sense- was: "I love you." The sound of what he said lingered in the temple hall.

Xi looked at him. "Pirouz go out the back entrance... you got what you came here for. Just go. By the time you leave the mountain, we will be enemies." Her tears returned, and she whispered, "I'm sorry, that's just how it is."

Pirouz winced, then nodded his head. He left the temple, using a tunnel that led to the other side of the mountain. He made his way to the bottom of the mountain. By the time he boarded a fishing boat at the foot of the mountain, they were enemies.

Jiao Long, Cong, and Zhang Li were impressed with the fact that Pirouz had survived, to say the least. They went down to a noodle house and listened to Pirouz recount the story. He omitted, however, the part where he apologized to Xi. His masters listened, enraptured by every word. All of them were thinking along the lines of the same thing. *The boy has survived, but he is still young, he has many more battles ahead of him!* Still, they kept these thoughts to themselves. Instead, they watched as their young student slurped up his noodles.

His shifus went back to their headquarters, leaving him alone. There was music coming from outside. Pirouz had another bowl, then another, then went outside to see the street performers. Crystal Sparrow spotted him as she balanced on her hands, legs twisting above her. She noticed Pirouz looking tired and beaten, though he had a smile on his face. He brought up the scarf she had forgotten, which made her smile.

After the show she approached him while her troop was packing their instruments into the wagon.

"Thank you for returning this." She said. "It means a lot to me." She regarded his beaten spirit, then asked: "What happened to you?"

Pirouz smiled wearily. "Does it matter?"

"No." She said while draping the scarf around her neck. "I suppose not."

The two walked around town in the midnight hour. They sat outside a tavern, a soft swarm of fireflies lighting up the night.

"Our troop is leaving town tomorrow morning," she said softly.

Pirouz responded with an exhausted "Oh?"

"Yeah... this can be a proper goodbye."

She placed her head on his shoulder and held his hand.

<u>ACKNOWLEDGEMENTS</u>

I would like to acknowledge and thank the following people: my brother Nader Astanboos, my sister-in-law Alexsandra, and lil' Eva. Doctor Mo Rafi and the Rafi family. Alex Rogers. My business partners April Mendoza and Chris Trull, the entire Wild 7 team. Lester & Lupe Trull, Louis & Edith Mendoza, Ashley Mendoza. Kory Squalls. Randy & Alexa Baptista, Maryon & Stephanie Baptista. Sergio Ramirez, Bernardo Lopez, Jason Linere White, Lucas Pitassi, the Debbie and the Devil gang. Rick Darge, Machete Bang Bang. Jessie Sanchez. Malina Galbova. Alex Gore. Lucas Eposito. Amoo Edik, Amoo Firouz, Amoo Yusef. Tye and Nicole. Rebecca Swenson. Hamide Hoseinzade. Zach Keyworth. Anthony Russel. Ali Sabet. Erfan. Josh Lavian. Nathan. Dax. Niloofar. Alex Deagon.Jesse Heisel. Stevie and Lucas. Ian Pons Jewell. Keita. Kim, Auntie Carol, and Darin Qualls. Cousin Phil Khozein. My artistic daughters Rocio Romero & Betsi Romero, Rozzibitsi. Joe Ide. Judd Apatow. Ron Yerxa. The darling Julie Hagerty. George Ross Satorino, Aaron Godfred. Dave Szamet. Trace De La Torre. Sara Mashayekh. Jacob Hunter. Marziyeh. Rouzbeh Parvin, Roza Parvin, Samad & Roya, my cousin Arash Milanizadeh, Armin: You showed me my first Bruce Lee film, I miss you cousin. Uncle Javad, Uncle Ali, Fareeba, Kiarash, Navid, Nima, & the kids. Danech Kiya, My dear Aunts & Uncles and many wonderful cousins in Iran. Raheleh Motebassem, Ramin Motebassem, Sean Larocca, Jason & Heidi Larocca. Brandon Forgo, Golnaz Saraaji, Jeiran, Elnaz, Tannaz, and Solmaz. Khaleh Shalah, Amoo Ali. Parker Clements. Salar, Soroush, Manoucher, & Raheleh. Cousin Hessam Joon, Sara, Hirad, and Ryan. Naz joon, Shayna, Naser, Amin and Mahnaz. Barney Black & Andrew Black. Baron Hats. Anna, Mars, and Zero. Dillon Terry. Hamid Reza Shaye, Khaleh Khateejeh, Malihe, Vahid, and Parham. Sharareh Frouzesh. Cheddar, Famous Blake. Shahram Khorram. Reza Khorram. Kiki Valentine. Lauren Norch. Paul Kreuger. Taylor Box. Dallas Schaefer. Trent Longo. Shannon Corbett. Derek Johnson. Ali Rashin and Elia. blkglfks. Carolina Alvarez, Lily Rangel, Morgan Andre, Dre Lamparello, Arezou and Todd and Arta and the fam, Rick Alves, Dean Cundey ASC, Casey Hartnett, Tuco El Buitre, Michael Jai White, Takato Yonemoto, Ryan Keem, Sean Wing, Jeremy Gaines. Kendall Ford. Jaime Ronquillo Jordan, Emmanuelle Medina. Lupe Solis. Charlie Bergum. Destiny Austin, Robert Bravo, Chris Candy, Film Junk, 3 Black Geeks. Kate Mara, Mahin Mansoob, Rudy Cartagena, Jabril, Muhammad, Lizz, Marjan Mahdizade, Judge Mathis,Alex Dayo, Alyun,Uncle Lloyd Kaufman, Adela, Alex Ingles, Tame Impala, Emily Selove. Young people of the world, run!
... And Zoe Rose.

ABOUT THE AUTHOR

Naz Red is a writer, director, animator, and occasional actor. He is responsible for the film Debbie and the Devil, the cartoon Turbo Hyper Commandos, and the comic book Killer Comanche. The House of Poison: Sword and Crystal Sparrow is his first novel.